"It's time for action n...

Oh, boy.

"Would you like a drink?" ...

fingers under the bodice of Frankie's dress, just there where the neckline angled from her shoulder to her breasts.

"I'm not very thirsty," she whispered.

Frankie's breath caught, her stomach tightening as heat coiled, hot and needy. She didn't know her moves here. Before, she'd just gone with the fantasy. But tonight?

This wasn't a fantasy, this was real.

Phillip hooked a finger in her dress, his knuckle sinking into her cleavage. His eyes locked on hers as he used it to pull her closer.

His lips were so close.

Then he brushed those lips over hers. Soft. So soft.

His tongue slid along the seam of her mouth, teasing one corner and then the other.

Delicious. So delicious.

His hands were warm on her back, his body hard against hers.

He leaned back, enough to look into her eyes. He must have liked what he saw there, because he nodded.

"Upstairs."

His quiet words weren't a question. She wasn't even sure they were a suggestion. To her body, they were a command.

One she couldn't refuse....

Blaze®

Dear Reader,

Don't you love the holidays? I do! I'm a total glutton for the season, everything from decorating to crafts to food... Oh, the food! To me, there is something magical about the season and I'm always excited to dive right in.

But Lieutenant Phillip Banks, my hero in *Christmas with a SEAL*, doesn't have that same love of the holidays. It's not that he hates them—he's simply indifferent. Enter Frankie Silvera, who is bound and determined to show Phillip the joy of the season and fill his heart with Merry. It made for a very interesting holiday for both of them, I think.

I hope you have a fun time with *Christmas with a SEAL*. Don't forget to check out my other Uniformly Hot! SEAL stories. You can see them all at www.tawnyweber.com/sexy-seals. I hope, too, that you have a fabulous holiday, filled with warm wishes, joyful memories and lots of great food!

Hugs,

Tawny Weber

Tawny Weber

—

Christmas with a SEAL

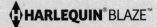
HARLEQUIN® BLAZE™

Recycling programs
for this product may
not exist in your area.

ISBN-13: 978-0-373-79823-0

Christmas with a SEAL

Printed in U.S.A.

ABOUT THE AUTHOR

A *New York Times* and *USA TODAY* bestselling author of over thirty hot books, Tawny Weber has been writing sassy, sexy romances since her first Harlequin Blaze book was published in 2007. A fan of Johnny Depp, cupcakes and color coordination, she spends a lot of her time shopping for cute shoes, scrapbooking and hanging out on Facebook.

Readers can check out Tawny's books at her website, www.tawnyweber.com, or join her Red Hot Readers Club for goodies like free reads, complete first chapter excerpts, recipes, insider story info and much more. Look for her on Facebook at www.facebook.com/tawnyweber.romanceauthor.

Books by Tawny Weber

HARLEQUIN BLAZE

COSMO RED-HOT READS FROM HARLEQUIN

To browse a current listing of all Tawny's titles, please visit www.Harlequin.com.

Big hugs to Helen Sibbrit and Kristin Betthauser
for a great title!
Thanks, sweethearts.

1

If she had a fairy godmother, Frankie Silvera would be sending her a big ol' thank-you bouquet for giving her the perfect opportunity to make some of her naughtiest dreams come true.

Or maybe it was her creative muse.

This was the kind of place that definitely inspired creativity. The Las Vegas penthouse was a kaleidoscope of sensations. Neon lights glinted off sparkling chandeliers, sending colorful sparkles over the crowd of partyers. Dressed in everything from sequins to plastic, denim to silk, bodies filled the room, covering the leather couches, perched on chrome stools around the horseshoe bar and flowing onto the dance floor.

Accentuating it all were intense music, free-flowing booze and men. So, so many men.

And, oh, baby, they were gorgeous.

It wasn't just knowing that most of these muscular, sexy men were Navy SEALs that made Frankie's insides dance. It was knowing that somewhere among them was her dream hottie and the answer to all of her problems.

She just had to find him.

"Frankie!"

Frankie had barely turned around before a pair of arms engulfed her.

"Lara, this is so fabulous." Frankie leaned back to take a good look at the other woman. "Not as fabulous as you, though. Wow, you look great."

Not a lie. Lara Banks had always been gorgeous. Tall and exotic with big green eyes and a body that made men drool. But today, she actually glowed. Her white satin dress was short and sassy, her auburn hair cut at a wicked angle and her Jimmy Choos put her a couple inches over six foot.

"You look good, too. Thank you for being here," Lara said, as if she really meant it.

Not that Frankie would blame her for just being polite. Despite having practically grown up in Lara's backyard, it wasn't as if the two women had been close. Lara's parents had been high-society snobs with very specific ideas of whom their children could associate with, and the granddaughter of their housekeeper wasn't on their list. Not that that would have mattered to Lara. But Lara had been totally absorbed in dance, running away at seventeen to dance on Broadway.

It wasn't until a few months back, when Lara paid her first visit to her family's estate in eight years, that the two women had gotten past that awkward "I know you but don't remember much more" stage.

"Thanks for inviting me to the wedding," Frankie said. "I have to say, when you do things, you definitely do them your way. This is amazing."

"I wouldn't be here if it wasn't for you," Lara murmured, pulling Frankie close for another hug.

"Sure, you would. I just got you drunk and let you talk," Frankie said with a laugh. All it'd taken was a bottle of Patron and a tray of Nana's brownies to finally break through Lara's defensive shell.

Frankie envied the woman, blown away by how much

in love she was with her SEAL. She liked to think she'd be able to pull that off someday. True love, happily ever after, lifelong sex. Maybe in a few years, after she'd reestablished her business, rebuilt her credit and lost five pounds.

Maybe.

"You were wonderful. A friend when I needed one." Lara squeezed Frankie's arms before stepping back and fingering her necklace. "And thank you for the early gift. It's my something new, but I'll be wearing it all the time."

Frankie tilted her head and tried to smile. A couple of years ago, she'd been celebrated in various circles, written up in magazines and on her way to building a stellar reputation as a gifted silversmith who specialized in quirky elegance. People had been lining up for her jewelry, and she'd been doing great. She'd had a fat contract from two national jewelers and more orders than she could handle. She'd invested in new equipment and leased a studio so she wasn't working out of her apartment. She'd even treated herself to a hot-off-the-showroom-floor Mini Cooper S convertible.

She'd had the dream. Then she'd blown it.

Nine months ago, she'd gotten *the dreaded block*.

All of her creative juices had dried up. Everything she made turned out hideous. She'd lost clients, she'd lost contracts, she'd lost her lease.

Six months ago she'd moved in with her grandmother.

Now she was making quirky customized Christmas ornaments to pay the bills. She'd told everyone she was exploring a new phase of art, when in reality all she wanted was what she'd had before.

She eyed the necklace, seriously proud of how it had turned out. With its edgy geometric shapes of copper, silver and bronze, it was perfect for Lara. Apparently she could only create great jewelry if she wasn't getting paid for it.

"Three of my dancer friends asked me if you'd be here," Lara said with a grin. "They all want you to design special pieces for them, too."

"I'm not doing jewelry anymore," Frankie demurred, trying not to sound bitter. For a while she'd hoped that her creativity would be like a feral cat, and if she pretended she wasn't interested it'd sneak up behind her.

It hadn't worked.

But Frankie was sure her plan tonight would.

"I told the girls you'd say that, but they're stubborn. Be prepared to fend off requests." Lara glanced around, then gave Frankie a wicked grin. "And not just for jewelry. You're catching a lot of looks, girly."

Frankie offered her trademark mischievous smile and twisted one red curl around her finger. She didn't need to look around to confirm that. A girl always knew when guys were checking out her ass.

"See anything you like?" Lara asked.

A room full of sexy guys with smoking-hot bodies? What wasn't to like?

They were enticing as hell, but if she was going to get wild, she only wanted one guy.

"I'm here to celebrate," Frankie said dismissively. "Not to hook up."

"You're in Las Vegas, Frankie. Go wild. Have fun." Lara laughed. "Don't forget, what happens in Vegas stays in Vegas."

"Tempting, but I'm not the wild Vegas type," Frankie told her, keeping her secret dream just that—secret. After all, she and Lara might have practically grown up together, but they weren't close enough for Frankie to share her hope of finding a guy she'd only seen a handful of times over the past ten years and seducing him.

Especially not when the guy was Lara's brother.

"You are so the wild type," Lara claimed, grabbing two glasses of champagne off a passing waiter's tray.

"Me? Wild?" Frankie pressed her hand to her chest and laughed before taking one of the glasses with a nod of thanks.

"Wasn't it you who was caught skinny-dipping in the high school swimming pool?" Lara sipped her bubbly and arched her brow. "You used to have blue hair and go to raves, right?"

"I just went for the dancing. And the blue seriously clashed with my freckles." Frankie grimaced. "But that's not wild. It just proves that I had questionable taste in hairstyles."

"Okay," Lara murmured. "So it wasn't you who constructed a metal elephant in the principal's office your senior year, led a protest against school lunches in sixth grade and had a childhood reputation for streaking."

Frankie pressed her lips together to hold back her giggle.

"Well, that streaking does show a wild side," she acknowledged. "Of course, I was three at the time."

She looked around the room, wondering if she could still pull it off. Granted, she wasn't three anymore, but she still had dimples on her butt. That had to be worth something.

"You work way too hard," Lara said, rubbing her hand over Frankie's shoulder. "Give yourself a break. Give yourself this weekend."

Frankie shook her head, forcing her smile to stay bright despite the tension spiking through her system. She'd spent the past six months feeling as if she were drowning and one day short of six months pretending she wasn't. So any acknowledgment of working too hard would ruin all of her well-developed pretending.

But the invitation to take the weekend?

That she'd be happy to take.

"Lara!"

Both women turned toward the makeshift stage at one end of the penthouse to see a gorgeous guy gesturing.

"Looks like Dominic wants to dance," Frankie said.

"You wanna come dance with us?" Lara offered, her eyes not leaving her man.

"You go," Frankie said. "Have fun."

"Stick around for cake," Lara said, not needing to be told twice. In a blink, the other woman was halfway across the room, making Frankie laugh.

Finishing her champagne, Frankie watched the happy couple get down and bust some impressive moves. She wanted that.

Not just someone to dance with, although a guy who could match her moves would be sweet.

What did it feel like to be in that kind of relationship? One where two people could block out a huge room full of partying people simply by looking into each other's eyes?

Frankie watched Dominic pull Lara into his arms, their bodies keeping perfect rhythm even as he lifted her hand to his lips to brush a kiss over her knuckles.

Sigh.

It was pure romance.

And not why she was here, Frankie reminded herself.

She wasn't looking for romance or forever after, like Lara had been.

She was looking for a very specific guy. The one she'd had a giant crush on as a preteen, the one who'd inspired all of her teenage fantasies and quite a few of her sexier adult ones.

The one who—she was positive—would turn everything around, if she could get him. Unlock her creativity and, with it, her confidence. Because lying to herself was only going to keep working for so long.

Accepting a second glass of liquid courage that tasted like champagne, she decided it was time to get to work on making this the best weekend of her life.

Not an easy task. She gave a soundless whistle, looking around. There were at least two hundred people here. Figuring it was a gift that all the guys were hot and sexy and made searching fun, she moved through the bodies to cross the room.

Whoa. Frankie narrowed her eyes, her heart picking up an extra beat and excitement dancing in her stomach.

Was that him?

She shifted to the right, trying to see around the crush of dancing bodies to the booths at the far end of the penthouse.

Oh…

Sitting alone in a booth and looking as though he wanted to be anywhere else but in that room, her dream guy was nursing a drink. His mahogany hair was shorn with military precision. A navy blue sweater covered his broad shoulders, emphasizing his perfect posture and, from what she could see, a gorgeous chest.

Phillip Banks.

He was even better looking now.

She didn't think they'd exchanged more than ten words her entire life. But she'd watched him. As a kid, because he looked like the heroes she read about in school. As a teen, because he looked like one of the actors on her favorite TV show. And as an adult, because he looked like a hottie who'd burn up the sheets. Most of her watching had been from afar whenever he visited his parents' house in Maryland.

But now, here he was. Up close and about to get personal.

And, oh, my, was he hot.

Nerves danced in her stomach. It was one thing to

dream about seducing her fantasy guy. She'd spent untold hours playing out the scenarios. She credited her artistic mind for the diverse variety of those scenarios, everything from Phillip staring at her blankly or laughing in her face to him looking at her with a combination of intrigue and desire in his eyes to—every once in a while, if she'd had an extra glass of wine—his confessing that he'd been lusting after her for years.

She knew that scenario was far-fetched given that the last time he'd seen her she had been fifteen and going through the bohemian stage of her search for her personal art style. She'd spent months wearing burlap, shunning shampoo and was usually covered in burns from the soldering iron she used to make her avant-garde metal sculptures.

But hey, maybe she'd get lucky.

In one form or another.

Frankie bounced across the floor in her beribboned Lucite heels, wondering if this was how Cinderella had felt when she'd spotted the prince at the ball.

Half delighted, half terrified.

And totally turned on.

STRIPPERS, BODY SHOTS, flashing lights and wild dancing.

Las Vegas at its finest.

Otherwise known as one of Lieutenant Phillip Banks's many versions of hell. Right up there with email spam, traffic jams and drug kingpins with a taste for exotic torture.

A man who believed in discipline, he made a point to do everything in his power to avoid the first two and take down the latter.

Especially the latter.

Phillip stared at his drink, slowly twisting the glass this

way, then that, while memories of his time as Valdero's unwilling guest flashed through his mind.

After he'd been captured on a mission gone wrong, it had taken his team three days to effect a rescue. In those three days, Phillip had experienced new levels of pain, discovered rage and reevaluated his beliefs about revenge.

For most of his life, his goal had been to be the best. To excel in all things—school, the military and the SEALs.

Now?

Now all he wanted was revenge on that sadistic son of a bitch, Valdero. And he planned to get it. He had the operation mapped out, he had a good idea who had sold out the team and he was ready to lead the mission to take Valdero down.

Phillip gulped his scotch with a grimace.

Hell, he'd even gone above and beyond the mandatory psych evaluation to ensure—and prove to those in command—that he was mentally capable of handling it.

He was ready.

Unfortunately, he was also in Las Vegas.

Frowning, Phillip looked around. He'd rather be in Coronado, studying strategy and perfecting his plan.

Under normal circumstances, he wouldn't think twice about doing an about-face and making for the nearest exit.

But this wasn't a normal circumstance.

This, God help him, was his sister's wedding.

A headache throbbing behind his left eye, he leaned his head against the back of the booth, watching the dancers wriggling all over the modified stage. He cringed when the leggy brunette in the middle did a wicked bump and grind.

"Helluva party," someone said, forcing Phillip to quit glaring at his dancing sister.

When he saw who was speaking, he automatically came to attention.

"Sir?"

"The party, it's the wildest wedding I've ever attended." Lieutenant Commander Blake Landon winced as the groom got up on stage, too, showing an impressive bump and grind of his own. "Although I'm pretty sure I didn't need to see that."

Wondering where he could get his eyeballs sandblasted, Phillip could only grunt his agreement.

"You're not celebrating?" Landon asked, dropping into the chair opposite Phillip so his back was turned toward the stage. Phillip would have preferred that spot if not for his policy to always sit with his back against a wall.

"I'm sure Lara considers my being here celebration enough," Phillip responded, figuring that and an appropriate wedding gift were really all anyone could ask of him.

"That was a good thing you did, giving the bride away."

Swirling the ice melting in his second scotch that night, Phillip could only shrug. A year ago—hell, six months ago—he'd been in what he considered peak form for a military officer. He'd trained hard, he was at the top of his game physically and mentally and he'd been completely unencumbered. He'd had no family to answer to, and his relationships with his fellow SEALs had been distant enough for him to do his job without any emotional baggage. And he'd been absolutely positive that he was on the right track.

And now?

He was reluctantly attending a tacky Las Vegas wedding with half of the SEAL platoon, his entire team and a sister he'd spent most of his life comfortably estranged from. And his right track? That had taken a sharp turn left.

"Sir?" he said, leaning forward, knowing his words would be easily drowned out by the loud music if anyone else were listening. "Any word on Candy Man?"

Landon's easy look faded at the mention of Valdero's

code name. His eyes went military hard and his demeanor shifted automatically.

"This isn't the time or the place," Landon said. "And you haven't been cleared for the mission. So until we're back on base, why don't you relax and enjoy your sister's happiness?"

Phillip clenched his teeth to keep his argument at bay, baffled at the unfamiliar fury surging through him. Apparently the extra therapy he'd gotten after the clear psych evaluation hadn't helped much. Before, he'd never gotten angry, never questioned orders. Yet here he was, ready to leap across the table, grab a superior officer and demand that he be allowed revenge.

Phillip tossed back the last of his scotch, wishing the alcohol would dull the hold those strange emotions had over him. He'd been called uptight most of his life, and he'd embraced that label. Reckless emotions were something he'd never indulged in.

Landon glanced over his shoulder, where the bride and groom were now slow dancing, in spite of the heavy bass ricocheting off the walls. "Give yourself a pat on the back for your part in bringing them together."

"That's all on them," Phillip said, wincing as the groom's hands slipped down to cup the bride's ass.

"Blake?"

Both men looked over and smiled. Phillip donned the polite society smile he'd been trained from birth to offer. Landon's smile was much sappier, the kind that said the guy was seriously crazy over his wife.

"Dance?" Alexia Landon asked, trailing her fingers over her husband's shoulder.

Landon nodded, and then gave Phillip a long look.

"Whether you want credit or not, from what I hear, the bride and groom are giving it to you," he told Phillip as he got to his feet. With that and a grin, he followed the leggy redhead onto the dance floor.

"Don't forget you have to stay until they cut the cake," the lieutenant commander threw over his shoulder.

Seriously?

Phillip eyed the clearly-not-ready-for-cake couple dancing on the stage, looked at his watch and raised his hand.

"Bartender?"

Thirty minutes and one scotch on the rocks over his two-drink limit later, his headache had spread to both eyes and was eking its way down the back of his neck. As he did with anything that didn't suit him, Phillip ignored it.

All he had to do was focus on his goal and push everything else from his mind. In this case, his goal was to get out of here. Less than a minute later, as he was plotting his escape, a woman dropped onto the banquette next to him.

Phillip blinked. Not in surprise, but in defense of his corneas. Was her dress made of mirrors? He squinted, realizing the tiny round tiles glittering their way over her curves were metal, not glass.

Did everything glitter in Las Vegas?

"Wow, this is wild," she said, waving her hand in front of her face to cool off. "Can you believe this place? I've never been in a penthouse before. Talk about doing it right."

She glanced over his shoulder as she said the words, her gaze taking in the neon landscape. Then, with a soft whistle, she gave him a wide-eyed look as if to say, *Wow.* Then she shifted, narrowing her gaze to focus on his face.

"You don't look like you're having fun," she observed, leaning closer. Close enough that her scent wrapped around him like a spicy hug.

"You look like you're having enough fun for both of us," he countered. He might be hating everything, but that was his problem. And there was something about this woman that made him want to smile, although he didn't know why.

"And guys like you don't like to have fun, is that it?" she asked, looking saucy.

"Guys like me?" Phillip dismissed with a laugh. "You don't know me, do you?"

"Sure, I do." She leaned close enough that he could count the freckles sprinkled across her nose and blink at how lush the lashes surrounding her deep brown eyes were.

"I hear you're Cupid."

Phillip grimaced.

"Not quite. Phillip Banks," he corrected automatically. As soon as the words were out he regretted them. Introductions led to conversation. Conversation led to connection, something he was anxious to eliminate.

"Hi, Phillip," she greeted with a laugh.

Phillip offered a distant nod, hoping she'd get the hint.

"This really is a great party, isn't it?" she said, not waiting for a response as she turned to check out the crowd. As she did, she twisted her riot of cinnamon curls around her fist and lifted her hair to cool the back of her neck.

Was that a tattoo on her neck? Not sure why he had to know, Phillip leaned forward to get a better look.

"Is that a bird?" he asked, squinting at the pale gray image.

"Hmm?" she murmured, turning back with a smile. She hadn't released her hair, so he could see the open-door cage, just a shade darker than the bird, tucked in the curve of her neck and shoulder. "It's freedom."

"What's freedom?"

"My bird," she explained. "It symbolizes flying free. You know, just like some of these guys probably have a bald eagle or something to symbolize freedom, I have a sparrow."

"They don't," he said without thinking.

She tilted her head to the side so her curls slid along her shoulders again, hiding her bird. "Don't what?"

"Most of them don't have tattoos," he explained reluctantly. He didn't like discussing the military with anyone who wasn't in it. But he'd brought it up, and it would be rude to ignore her question. "Most of the guys here are SEALs. Identifying marks can be detrimental to their careers."

"They're against the rules?"

"No. Just not smart." Phillip knew there were plenty of tattooed SEALs. He'd served with a few. But every member of the team went on a mission with no ID, no tags, no personal effects for a reason. Phillip had seen what a mission gone wrong could do. Hell, the memory still played out in Technicolor every night when he closed his eyes.

"I'll bet you are," the redhead said, pulling his attention out of the past. When she leaned forward on her elbows to give him a thorough look, the move sent her mirrored tiles swinging.

"You bet I'm what?"

"Smart."

Phillip blinked. He used to think he was. Now? He had no idea.

"I'm Frankie." She thrust out her hand, her smile widening. "It's great to see you."

"It's nice to meet you," Phillip said automatically, taking her hand. He was surprised at how small and delicate it was.

Her lips pursed, the move making him uncomfortably aware of how full her mouth was.

"You don't know me, do you?" she stated, her brown eyes dancing with mirth.

"Should I?" Yes, his tone was stiff. He didn't like people laughing at him, and he was sure that was exactly what the redheaded sprite was doing.

"I'm a friend of Lara's."

Of course she was.

Phillip was sure the room could be divided into two camps.

The wild, gyrating, tattooed camp his sister belonged to.

And the protocol-loving, rule-living camp of the Navy that he thrived in.

Why, oh, why, did the two have to converge?

The pretty redhead shifted a little closer. Her dress showed off her golden shoulders and deep cleavage, and the table didn't block the length of her long, silky legs beneath her short skirt.

Sexual awareness hit hard and fast and very unwelcome.

In defense against it, Phillip looked away. His gaze landed on the stage, where his sister and Castillo were wrapped around each other like vines. It was Lara's hand on her husband's ass this time.

"Good God." A waiter approached the table and Phillip gratefully exchanged his empty glass for a full one, giving the guy a smile and a signal to keep them coming. If this kept up, he was going to need a few more.

He fought the desire to simply get up and leave. To get the hell out of here. But he was trapped. Trapped by his emotions, by the sudden demands of family, by his memories.

Desperate for distraction, a part of him screaming for reprieve, Phillip focused all of his considerable attention on Frankie. The name chimed faintly in his memory, but the sound was easily drowned out by his third scotch.

"C'mon," Frankie said, getting to her feet and reaching out to grab his hand.

"Where?" Phillip didn't get up, but he didn't shake off her hand either. There was something oddly compelling about her touch. That, and seeing her standing there, her short dress glistening and her hair swirling around her face, was a serious turn-on.

"The dance floor, of course," she said, laughing. "You can't tell me you're Lara's brother and you don't dance."

The waltz, a foxtrot if forced and—although he'd only admit it at gunpoint—the tango, all thanks to lessons mandated by his mother, the queen of high society. Phillip glanced at the dancers and shook his head. Not one lesson at Madame Lenore's had included a bump or a grind. He'd be lost out there.

"C'mon," Frankie said again, tugging.

Curious, and just a little bit fascinated, Phillip let her drag him to his feet. Her tiny hand wrapped around his, she pulled him through the dancers. She was so small he felt as though he should be the one in front, protecting her. But she moved like a friendly bulldozer, her smile parting the crowd all the way to the sliding glass door that led to the patio. And, he knew from his initial inspection, a private elevator.

Escape.

"I'm staying until cake." He grimaced, remembering Landon's orders.

She grabbed a bottle of champagne from a passing waiter and handed it to him before taking two empty glasses with a murmured thanks.

"Cake isn't for another half hour," she said with a wink, pushing the door open and leading him through. It silently slid shut behind them and then—blessed quiet.

Phillip closed his eyes for a second, letting the lack of wailing guitars wash over him. It wasn't until his ears stopped ringing that he realized there actually was music out here, too. Softer music. A medley of strings.

"Dance?" Frankie asked, setting the glasses on an empty table.

Phillip hesitated.

Not because he didn't want to dance with her.

But because he did.

This was the wrong time to be attracted to a woman.

His head was all kinds of messed up. He was on a personal mission for vengeance.

He didn't do relationships. And despite her party-girl appearance, there was something about her freckles that told him Frankie was a relationship girl at heart.

Which made her off-limits.

Relationships and a career as a Navy SEAL? Despite the celebrating going on in the other room, Phillip knew relationships were a bad idea. He didn't believe in splitting his focus, and had long ago vowed that his only commitment would be to his career.

He'd be better off making his excuses and returning to the noisy assault and painful visuals. Ready to do just that, he gave Frankie a polite smile.

And wished those huge brown eyes weren't so appealing. Or that body so temptingly hot.

But those huge brown eyes *were* so appealing, and that body *was* temptingly hot. Her personality was so damned engaging that, for the first time since he'd been taken captive, he didn't feel lost. The vicious fury that had become his constant companion, and that no therapy could erase, was shoved aside.

Instead, lust took over.

2

FRANKIE HELD HER BREATH, her heart beating so hard she was surprised her dress wasn't shaking. Eyes wide, she waited to see what he'd do. After a second he glanced at the door leading back to the party. She tried not to pout, sure he was about to refuse.

Then, with a small frown, he set down the champagne bottle and held out a hand.

Look at how he made that look as if it was his idea. She grinned as she placed her hand in his and let him lead her out of view of the door. Of course, Phillip Banks of the Maryland Bankses was high society through and through.

Kinda like a prince.

Which, given her status in that same state, made her a pauper.

She wiggled her toes in her beribboned Lucite heels, figuring she could rock the role of Cinderella for just one night.

They reached the far side of the patio, a bronze fire pit casting a magical glow over them as Phillip faced her, his hand curling around her waist.

Amusement fled.

So did thought.

All Frankie could do was feel.

Staring into Phillip's brilliant green eyes, she gave over to delight, loving everything that was going on in her body as they began to sway to the music.

Excitement.

Curiosity.

And a sexual rush that was doing wild things to her insides.

Tingling things. Wet, hot things.

Things that made her wonder what it would be like to strip naked and see what other moves he had.

The music picked up and Phillip's arched brow was her only warning before he twirled her out and then pulled her back into his arms.

Oh, baby.

"I'm impressed. You have to have a special kind of rhythm to move like this," she said with a breathless laugh. "I guess dance lessons do pay off."

"You say that as if you know me," he noted quietly, his gaze intent.

She opened her mouth to tell him she did before closing it again. Just because she knew him didn't mean he knew her. She wasn't sure they'd ever actually said more than hello to each other before tonight.

Admitting how she knew him would mean telling him she was little Francesca Silvera, the housekeeper's granddaughter. The tomboy who'd had a secret crush on him all the way through school. Who'd endured haystack hair for a year after dying her red curls blonde to try to look more like his prom queen girlfriend. She'd been the laughingstock of the sixth grade.

Hey, a girl needed some secrets, right? It wasn't as if he was ever going to come back to the Banks estate and find out who she really was. So why shouldn't she enjoy the encounter for what it was—two people, practically strangers, who were very attracted to each other. At least, she was very attracted to him.

Phillip was hard to read.

"Frankie?" he prompted, his voice a little huskier than before.

"You've got a polish that most guys only have if they've taken lessons," she lied, giving him a saucy look. "On top of that, you definitely move like a man who knows what to do with his body."

"Are you flirting with me?" he asked, sounding baffled.

Delighted, she laughed. Poor guy. He clearly hadn't been flirted with enough in his privileged lifetime if he had to ask.

"Do you mind if I do?"

A tiny frown creased his brow. Before he could resolve whether he minded or not, Frankie decided to tilt the odds in her favor. She moved a little closer, her fingers sliding from his shoulder to skim along the back of his neck.

She wet her lips, smiling a little when his gaze shifted. She'd spent many a teenage year dreaming of him looking at her this way. At first she hadn't had a clue what she'd do if he did give her that look. But thanks to the library, HBO and three older female cousins, it wasn't that long before she could fill in all the juicy details of her fantasy.

And life had just handed her a golden opportunity to live out that fantasy, to get more specific about those details. She knew she would regret it if she didn't make the most of it.

"I don't think flirting is a good idea," he told her, his voice deep.

"Oh, I beg to differ," she said, sliding closer. Her breasts brushed his chest, but thanks to the material of her dress, all she felt was hard metal instead of the hard expanse of his sexy chest. So she shifted, pressing one thigh between the length of both of his. Oh, the delight. "Never discount the fun of flirting."

"Fun?"

"You don't think flirting is fun?"

He looked so serious as he considered her question.

"Flirting is usually a prelude," he mused, his fingers flexing on her hip. Frankie wondered if he wanted to slide them down, wished he would. She'd love to feel his hand on her butt. Would he grab and squeeze, or smooth and caress?

"A prelude to what?" she asked, her thumb circling his palm. His slacks rubbed in delicious friction against the inside of her bare thigh.

"A prelude to trouble," he decided with a smile, looking as if he was trying to warn her off but didn't want to be rude.

Ever the gentleman. Enjoying the feeling of his leg between hers, Frankie smiled. She'd always wondered if she could tempt him to lose that polite sheen. Time to find out.

"You consider sex trouble?" she asked, her fingers skimming up and down the warm skin along the back of his neck. At the same time, she gave him her sultriest look—practiced for hours in front of her bedroom mirror—and made a show of nibbling on her bottom lip.

His eyes narrowed, but his expression didn't change. She was impressed. She'd only used that look on one guy before—and granted, he'd been delivering her new futon and she'd been trying to convince him to take the old couch away—but the result had been positive. He'd hauled off the couch, set up her futon and even moved her entertainment center.

But Phillip was a military man. A Navy SEAL. A yummy challenge in the form of her dream guy. Excitement layered over desire.

He was the answer to everything she needed.

A sexy lover she'd been fantasizing about for most of

her life. A hot, exciting man who, she was sure, in just one night would set her inspiration free.

If Frankie could seduce a man as controlled as Phillip Banks, she knew she could seduce her own creative muse out of the cave it had been hiding in.

"I consider anything done impetuously to have the potential for trouble," Phillip said quietly, his words reminding her of the teasing question she'd asked. "Sex between strangers is both impetuous and ill-advised."

Ill-advised? Frankie's lips twitched. He was so cute and proper.

"Well, then, why don't we get to know each other?" she suggested, her fingers trailing along the back of his neck. "I'm Frankie. I work with silver, love pasta and hoard cookbooks, even though I can barely boil water."

He looked baffled for a second, and then his eyes dropped to her dress. Since he had to look past the ample curves of her breasts to see it, she bit her lip, watching to see his reaction.

Nothing. She frowned.

Then his eyes met hers again and heat exploded in her belly.

Oh, those eyes. Deep green, filled with as much passion as pain. She wanted to pull him tighter into her arms and make him forget everything except pleasure.

"Silver? Like jewelry?"

Frankie's stomach clenched, the familiar knot of fear thrumming in her chest. She'd always wanted to be an artist. To stand out for her creative style and share her vision with others. Until that vision had faded.

The answer to blocked creative energy was to refill the well. She'd tried every other option. Yoga, creative play dates with herself, changing her diet, her sleep habits and her hairstyle. Nothing had helped.

She took a deep breath, focusing on Phillip's face. On

his steady gaze. He'd help. He was the only fantasy she'd ever had that she hadn't lived out. As soon as she did, she was sure the block would be broken.

"There are a lot of other things made of silver besides jewelry," she finally said, smiling sassily. "Quirky, fun, out-of-the-box things. Art's more fun when it's unexpected, don't you think?"

She almost laughed aloud at the look on his face. Polite doubt. Then his eyes slid down her face like a gentle caress, pausing for a second on her lips before dipping lower.

Oh. Her breath caught, her body happily sliding back over to the desire side, closing the door on all her boring doubts and worries. No, being turned on was much more fun.

Even more fun?

Turning Phillip on.

Hoping she could, Frankie took a deep breath, letting the cool air work its magic on her breasts, pressing them closer to his chest.

His eyes met hers, desire clear in the green depths.

"Did you make your dress?" he asked, sounding so normal she had to blink and wonder if she'd misread that look.

She shifted so her thigh rubbed against his, her hip brushing the front of his slacks. Heat exploded in her belly, sending awareness through her body.

He might sound indifferent, but he was rock hard.

So she could listen to his tone, or something else.

The choice was a no-brainer.

"I didn't make the dress, no. If I had, I'd have made sure it was a little more secure," she said, shrugging one shoulder so the strap slipped just a little. "It's heavy and it's so loose on top that I'm sure one wrong move and the whole thing will end up on the floor."

Or one right move.

Phillip looked as though she'd smacked him upside the

head. His eyes went dark and his breath caught as the image took hold.

Frankie pressed her tongue against her upper lip, enjoying his reaction.

"So now you know about me. Tell me about you and then we won't be strangers anymore."

"There's nothing to tell."

"No? I must have misunderstood," she teased, not wanting to give away why she really knew so much about him. Tell a guy you knew he wore boxers and size-thirteen boots and liked his waffles with chopped bananas and he'd be bound to get crazy ideas and call her a stalker. "So you're not a SEAL? You have no stories about growing up with Lara? You don't have any hobbies or interests?"

His lips quirked.

"I am a SEAL, and what I do tends to be classified. If I told stories about Lara, she'd likely tell some about me. I don't remember any embarrassing ones, but I'm sure she can. And no, I don't have any hobbies."

His hands shifted from her waist to cup her hips, his fingers brushing the top curve of her butt.

"And interests?" Frankie asked, her words just above a whisper.

"Right now my only interest is you," he confessed quietly, his body moving against hers in time with the melody coming from the outdoor speakers.

"See, this kind of trouble, it's good," she told him, surprised she could even form words. Her heart was racing, her pulse dancing way too fast for the music. Her stomach was knotted, but she was too overwhelmed to tell if it was nerves or excitement.

"You think so?" he asked as his lips brushed over hers. Soft, so gentle that she almost whimpered at the sweetness. And almost groaned when he pulled away.

Oh, yeah. He was worth the trouble. Her breath a little

shaky, Frankie leaned back to stare at Phillip, trying to gauge his thoughts. Or, more important, his decision on whether she was worth the trouble.

"Wanna leave?" She figured she'd better do the asking, since she knew he wouldn't.

Good guys, proper guys like Phillip, they didn't suggest one-night stands with women they thought were strangers. She'd wondered if his years in the Navy had changed that. She was glad it hadn't, but man, it would've been so much easier if he just grabbed her and dragged her away.

Since he wouldn't, she decided she would.

"Come on," she insisted, ignoring the chill as she stepped out of his arms and grabbed his hand. She turned toward the elevator, but her feet were frozen to the floor.

"Frankie..."

If she hesitated, he'd say goodbye. He'd go back inside, say goodbye and that would be it. She wet her lips, tasting him.

She wanted him even more now than she'd ever dreamed she could. But nowhere in her imagination had she fantasized about dragging him off to sexual nirvana. It was a little unnerving. But not once in any of her fantasies had she chickened out.

So...

"Come on," she said again, tugging his hand. She stopped to grab their glasses and what was left of the champagne, then tilted her head toward the elevator.

"Let's see how exciting trouble can be," she suggested.

"This isn't a good idea," Phillip murmured, looking back at the party as though he might actually consider joining the conga line to escape.

"Why?" Frankie asked, coming around to face him, so close the metal disks of her dress were probably leaving an imprint on both of their bodies.

"I'm not a relationship kind of guy," he warned huskily, his gaze locked on his fingers as they trailed down her cheek, over her chin and along her throat.

"I'm not looking for a relationship," she told him quietly, taking his hand in hers and pressing it against the curve of her breast above her dress.

No. She didn't want the prince forever.

She just wanted him for one hot night.

PHILLIP RACKED HIS BRAIN, wondering where the hell logic, caution and good sense had gone. Because, like Elvis, they had clearly left the building.

For once, though, he didn't care.

For the first time in months, he felt alive.

Loosed from the vicious grip of memories, his body celebrated its freedom by reminding him of all the reasons it felt great to be a man. Most of them below the belt and all of them quite happy to follow Frankie into that elevator.

So why was he hesitating?

He glanced at the party in the penthouse again, and closed his eyes. That was why. Family expectations, polite behavior and orders all demanded that he go back in there.

All his life, he'd met expectations, behaved appropriately and complied with demands before they were issued. He lived for orders, had been groomed to issue them. His entire life was a lesson in discipline.

And he was so damned tired of it.

He looked at Frankie, watching the way the neon from the Vegas night sky played over her hair. Her eyes were like midnight, dancing with the same delight that played out over her full lips. She was sexy, so temptingly sexy.

It wasn't that he went through life ignoring temptation; he'd simply trained himself not to see it. But there was no denying that he saw her, in all her tempting glory. His gaze shifted from Frankie's face, drifting down her body. Curves that even a dress of mirrors couldn't detract from.

And those legs. Phillip's eyes shifted to take in their long, golden length. Would they feel as silky as they looked? She was on the short side, but her legs were so long. Long enough, he'd bet, to wrap around his waist.

Want hit him hard, hotter and faster than he'd ever felt before. *Lust* was the only word for it. *Desire* was too tame, *passion* too soft. This was edgy, needy, demanding.

Way too much for that simple kiss they'd shared.

Because his profession—and his personality—demanded accuracy, he needed to find out.

Was it really lust?

Or was it all in his head?

His gaze locked on hers, Phillip stepped closer. Her dress jingled and her lips parted. He took her mouth. This kiss was soft, too. A brush of the lips, sweet and tasting of champagne. He shifted the angle, his tongue sliding along the seam of her mouth.

It was as if he'd flipped a switch.

Hers, his, he had no idea.

But the kiss went wild.

She nipped at his bottom lip.

His tongue demanded entrance, thrusting, swirling, taking. Giving. Tiny explosions, a minefield of emotional bombs, burst inside him. He couldn't think, couldn't focus.

He could only feel, taste. Want.

Oh, God, he wanted.

Frankie's arms wrapped around him, one across his shoulder so the champagne bottle she still held smacked him in the back. The other slid lower, her hand cupping, squeezing his butt.

Phillip wanted to reciprocate.

He wanted to touch her. To feel her skin beneath his palms, under his mouth.

But not here.

Somewhere private.

Because once he started, he wasn't going to be able to stop.

He didn't care whether it was lust alone or a temporary escape from the soul-deep exhaustion that had been eating way at him.

She was the answer to the question he couldn't face.

A question that was tearing at his heart, cutting at his soul.

He knew the answer was temporary.

He didn't care.

For one night, he wanted—needed—what she could give him.

Unable to resist, he backed her up against the elevator door, his hands diving into her soft cloud of hair, holding her head steady so he didn't have to release her mouth.

He stabbed the call button, then lost himself in the delight of her until the doors slid open.

"Inside," he said, guiding her into the car without taking his mouth from hers. He pressed her against the elevator wall as the doors closed, only letting go of her long enough to punch his floor number.

Their tongues danced, sliding over each other in the same seamless rhythm in which their bodies had moved to the music.

His brain was blessedly blank, all of his senses focused solely on Frankie. On how she felt. On how she made him feel.

Incredible.

Then she gently took his hand from her hair, sliding it down her face, over her throat. She didn't stop until his knuckles were brushing the soft flesh of her breasts, just where her dress started.

Phillip barely bit back a groan, his fingers itching to touch more. To slip beneath her dress and feel her skin, to rub his thumb over her nipple and feel it bead beneath his flesh.

But they were in an elevator. And he was only three floors down.

Then Frankie shrugged, proving once again that her dress wasn't fitted. The heavy fabric slid off her shoulder, the strap catching on her elbow.

And baring one breast.

He hated to leave the delicious haven of her lips, but he had to look. Just had to.

With one last slide of his tongue over her lower lip, he leaned back, his eyes dropping.

Holy hell, she was gorgeous.

Milky pale, with a glistening of freckles, her breast was full, the tip light coral, beaded and begging.

Unable to resist, he brushed the tip of his finger over her nipple.

Her breath caught on a whimper.

He heard a ding, vaguely realizing they'd reached his floor.

But he couldn't stop touching her. Couldn't resist rubbing the pebbled velvet again. He felt her breath catch against his lips and reveled in her reaction. Power, intense and gratifying, surged through him. Her fingers dug into his arms, kneading, then soothing.

He heard a vague ding again as he slid his lips down the slender length of her neck, breathing in her scent. Flowers and moonlight, sweet and mysterious. He wanted to lose himself in her.

"More," she murmured, her hands shoving at his waist to get beneath his sweater. Her fingers were like fire on his skin, making him want things he'd never wanted before. Making him need things he'd never imagined.

"Much more," she purred as his lips skimmed down her

shoulder. His hand was on the strap of her dress, ready to push it down and feast, when he heard a loud bang.

Phillip's lust cleared instantly, his body curving protectively over Frankie's as his senses took inventory.

Elevator, hotel, Las Vegas.

His adrenaline leveled.

His lust surged.

Lust he wasn't going to slake in a damned elevator.

Phillip wasn't sure how they made it to his room without invoking any public-indecency laws. Of course, the laws for that kind of thing might be different in Las Vegas.

He had no idea how he found his key card; he didn't remember getting it or opening the door to his hotel room. He just knew that in less than a minute after leaving the elevator, the room door was slamming shut behind him.

Frankie sauntered ahead, her swinging hips making her dress jingle.

"Champagne?" she offered, giving him a teasing smile over her shoulder and holding up the half-empty bottle.

"I'm not thirsty," he said, stripping his sweater over his head and tossing it on the floor. "I'm hungry."

She turned around, her eyes glazing over as her gaze moved across his chest. He liked her reaction. The way her pupils dilated, her breath quickened.

"What are you hungry for?" she asked, her words husky and low.

"Trouble."

Frankie's laugh rang through the room, the sound filling him with delight and a weird sort of joy. Instead of trying to figure out why, he ignored it. After all, there were much more interesting things to do tonight than analyze his feelings.

"Well, I'm the girl for you, then," she said. Her smile was both cute and seductive as she set the bottle on the bedside table. Her eyes locked on his and she stepped forward. Not close enough for him to touch, and just far enough from him to make it clear that he was supposed to wait.

Phillip didn't know if he could.

"Music?" Frankie asked huskily.

"You're kidding, right?"

"Yeah," she said, laughing and doing that little shoulder wiggle. "I'm kidding."

He barely heard her words through the roaring in his head. Blood surging south, he figured.

Because her dress had finally finished the journey it had been attempting all night and hit the floor.

Leaving Frankie standing in a tiny pair of silver mesh panties and high heels.

And Phillip ready to explode.

3

FRANKIE WAS GIFTED with a vivid imagination and an active fantasy life. She'd imagined seducing Phillip a million times. She'd spent endless hours fantasizing about him seducing her. She'd dedicated countless orgasms to the cause.

She wanted this.

She'd been dreaming about it, hoping for it, planning for it, even.

Yet now that she was standing in front of Phillip in all her naked glory, she was trembling in her high heels. Part of it was unquestionably desire. But there, beneath the excitement, was fear. What if this didn't break her creative block? What if she was doomed never to make anything original again? Or worse, what if the sex was so amazing, she wanted more? What if he was so amazing, he became more than a fantasy?

The closer Phillip stepped, the faster her pulse raced. But it still couldn't keep up with the tangled thoughts speeding through her head.

So she did what any smart woman on a quest for pleasure would do. She ignored the fear and focused on the desire.

Which got easier the closer Phillip came. His green eyes were hot, his look intent as it roamed her body. Figuring tit deserved tat, her gaze shifted. Oh, baby, his shoulders were so deliciously broad. He didn't have a bodybuilder's physique; he was too slender for that. But his sculpted muscles were a testament to the physical demands of his career. His skin was pale gold, his chiseled chest covered with a dusting of dark hair.

Frankie's fingers itched to touch it, to know if it was silky or crisp. She wanted to slide her hands over those arms and see if her hands could even fit around those impressive biceps. Her eyes drifted lower, following the trail of hair to his slender waist and, dammit, his slacks.

She wanted him naked. She wanted to see if the rest of him was as delicious as what she'd seen so far.

She raised her gaze to his face, ready to demand that he drop his drawers and put them on equal footing—nudity-wise.

But then she saw the look in his eyes.

He looked fascinated. As if she were the answer to something, something he desperately needed. Her breath caught, her heart clenching at whatever was beneath that look. Then he met her gaze.

"You're like something out of a dream," he murmured. He reached out, just one finger, and skimmed it over the curve of her breast.

Frankie barely kept from whimpering. She was pretty sure melting into an orgasmic puddle at the first touch would blow her sophisticated facade. Besides, she wanted more.

So much more.

Whisper soft, his finger traced a circle around her nipple.

Desire, sharp and needy, blasted through her, exploding in all the right places. She curled her toes to try to keep from falling out of her shoes.

Her breath came out in a surprised "Oh."

How could such a simple touch feel so good in so many places? Her knees trembled, and she squeezed her thighs together to intensify the pleasure building in her core. She wet her lips. She'd planned to tell him what she liked, how she liked it. But she had a feeling that he'd find so many new ways to pleasure her, ones she'd never even imagined.

As if reading her thoughts and ready to prove her right, Phillip flicked his thumb over her nipple. Then, before she could even murmur her approval, he pinched it between two fingers, still rubbing with his thumb.

Desire spiraled in a tight coil, filling her core with wet heat. Excitement built as sensations bombarded her. His thumb was rough, his palm warm. Color exploded against her closed eyelids, the miniorgasm rocking her body.

She shuddered with pleasure. But it wasn't enough.

She wanted more.

She needed more.

Her hands raced over his body. He was so hard, so deliciously hard. Done waiting, she skimmed her hands over his rock-hard abs, delighting for only a second before grappling with his belt buckle and ripping at his slacks. They had to go. She had to feel him.

"Hurry," she demanded, shoving his pants off his hips. She felt him kick them away, but didn't have time to do more than suck in a breath before he had her against the wall. His hands gripped hers, pulling her arms over her head. His mouth raced over her throat, down her chest. When he sucked her nipple between his teeth, Frankie bucked against him.

Her fingernails dug into her palms as she strained against his grip, wanting to touch, needing to give him the same pleasure he was offering her.

"We shouldn't be doing this. It's crazy," he muttered, pulling away. Thankfully not too far, though. Just enough for Frankie to see his face.

Her breath knotted in her chest. She tried to swallow, but it took her three attempts before air hit her lungs.

It wasn't the idea that he would call it quits before they finished what they had started that made her want to cry. It was the look in his eyes.

There was so much pain in those green depths, and it was buried so deep that she wondered if he even acknowledged it. It tore at her heart, making her want to pull him close and soothe him. To offer her shoulder, to find a way to heal him.

But she knew he wouldn't accept it.

Her goal tonight had been to heal her broken imagination. To use her fantasy as a key to reopen her creative doors.

Now all she wanted was to make Phillip feel better than good. She wanted him to feel incredible. So incredible that he forgot those secrets tearing at his soul. So incredible that he found peace.

So incredible that he never forgot her.

"Why is it crazy to feel good?" she asked, finally responding to his comment.

She saw the response in his eyes before he said a word. That rigid control of his was shoving aside the passion, replacing it with logic. Talk about crazy.

Frankie pressed her finger against his lips before he could voice his thoughts. She shook her head, giving him her sexiest look.

"You do make me feel good, Phillip. So good. The way you touch me, it's getting me excited. Thinking about what's coming next, it's making me so hot." She rubbed her finger over his bottom lip, her eyes locked on his as she stretched to brush a kiss over that lip. She arched her brow, then without warning, gave him a gentle nip.

He hissed. His fingers tensed on her hips, as if he

couldn't decide whether to push away from her or pull her closer.

She figured it was the least she could do to help him figure it out.

She moved her hand down so both palms were on his chest, circling, caressing.

"You want me," she told him, sliding one hand lower to cup the hard length of him pressing against her thigh. "You can have me. All you have to do is let go. Quit worrying. Quit thinking. Just feel."

Brows furrowed, he looked as if he didn't understand. Had he never let go? Never let himself be free?

Suddenly desperate to give him that, Frankie ran her tongue over his lip. When his eyes glazed, she gave his lip another little nip, then sucked it into her mouth and soothed the flesh with her tongue. At the same time, she curved her fingers around his erection, squeezing gently as she rubbed her thumb over the velvety tip.

He growled, shifting so their bodies were pressed together, her hand trapped between them.

One hand tunneled into her hair, tilting her head, his tongue sweeping past hers to take over the kiss. Even as his mouth sent her reeling with desire, she was blown away by his tenderness.

His other hand swept down, his fingers skimming over her skin so softly that she shivered. He cupped her breast, gently weighing its fullness while teasing the tip. Heat curled tighter, wet and needy between her thighs.

Frankie wrapped her leg around his, curling her foot behind his thigh to pull him closer, to press her aching core against his heat.

Suddenly, before she even realized he'd moved, Phillip was kissing his way down her body. His hand still cupping her breast, he sucked one nipple into his mouth. Frankie gasped as pleasure shot through her body.

Then she stiffened, every one of her senses going on full alert as his fingers slipped along the elastic of her panties. She could still feel everything else he was doing, and it was all making her crazy with desire. But it was all going on in the background, while center stage was his hand, her panties and what came next.

She was pretty sure that it would be her.

His finger slipped under the silky fabric.

She held her breath.

Ever so gently, he touched her swollen bud.

Frankie gasped. Need coiled tighter within her.

She was so close, the edge of delight within reach. She could feel it, the key to everything she wanted, dancing there on the tip of his fingers.

But she couldn't go over, couldn't let herself. Not until she knew he was right there with her, free from those demons she'd seen in his eyes.

"Are you letting go?" she asked, her words coming in pants. "Are you feeling, just feeling?"

"I feel you," he said, the words themselves as exciting as the feel of his mouth brushing over her nipple as he said them. "I promise the only thing in my mind right now is you. How you feel. How you taste. How much I want you."

Frankie whimpered, not knowing how she managed to hold back the orgasm those words inspired.

"I want you to want me so much you can't think at all," she said, shifting the hand trapped between them so she could touch him again. As if anticipating her move, he shifted.

Sliding his body down hers, every delicious inch of him skimming her body on his way down, he dropped to his knees at her feet. His hand still worked her breast, even as he lifted one of her legs and draped it over his shoulder.

Frankie's breath hitched as she anchored her shoulders against the wall, watching in fascination as Phillip pressed tiny kisses along her inner thigh. Each one a little higher than the other until he reached her throbbing core.

She wanted to watch. She needed the visuals for future fantasies. But the sensations were too overpowering.

Her eyes closed as his tongue swept along her bud, sipping, then sucking.

His fingers, one, two, slipped inside.

Moving.

Swirling.

Plunging.

"Go," he demanded.

The command, the vibrations of his words against her flesh, the feel of his breath.

She couldn't take it. She couldn't stop herself.

She flew over the edge.

Oh, wow.

Colors and shapes exploded behind her closed eyes, her head falling back against the wall. The climax pulsed through her in waves of pleasure. Her heart pounded so loudly, she could barely hear her labored breathing.

Wow.

When he let go, he really let go.

SHE TASTED LIKE AMBROSIA.

Healing, delicious nectar.

Phillip's head swam with the power of their passion. He'd never felt this before. Never wanted to. The idea that one person could take over every sensation in his body, could command his complete attention?

He'd have said it was impossible.

But as Frankie trembled, her cries of delight filling his ears, Phillip had to admit, he'd been wrong.

"In me," she panted. "I want you inside me."

"Can't." His words were a grunt, his fingers gripping the soft flesh of her butt, his lips pressed to her silken belly as he breathed in her scent and grappled for control. "No condom."

"Shoe."

"I beg your pardon?" Phillip frowned, opening one eye to peer up at her to see if she'd bumped her head in all the excitement.

"My shoe," she repeated. She didn't look impaired, unless absolutely satisfied counted.

Phillip would have preened a little at the look on her face, but he was too confused.

"You want me to use your shoe?"

Frankie's laugh was breathless and light, her hand curving over his cheek before sliding it through his hair in a way that was both exciting and comforting at the same time.

"They are sexy shoes," she acknowledged. "And they have a tiny pocket under the ribbons."

If he'd been fascinated by her before, he was now in complete awe.

His fingers skimming down the gentle curve of her calf, he curled his palm over her ankle for a moment before skimming his fingers lower to find the pocket.

"You have a condom in your shoe?" His laugh was a puff of warm air against her belly.

"Another in the other shoe," she told him, finally lifting her head to offer a sassy smile. "Shall we put them to good use?"

Having been raised a gentleman, Phillip knew it'd be churlish to disappoint a lady. Especially one standing over him in all her naked glory.

In thirty seconds flat, he had her condomless shoes off, and her naked body on the floor beneath his. A part of him demanded that he slow down, carry her to the bed.

But he couldn't wait that long.

"Now," she demanded, in perfect sync.

"Now," he agreed, sheathing himself.

Oh, God. Phillip thrust into Frankie's welcoming heat. It felt like coming home, to a home he'd never known. A delicious home. A hot, wet home.

Her fingers dug into his shoulders, her heels pressed tight against the small of his back.

She met every thrust with a small cry.

She was on the edge.

Phillip wanted her to go over.

This time, he needed to watch her go over.

As if reading his thoughts, Frankie pressed both hands against his chest, forcing him to pause.

"Feel," she demanded breathlessly.

She wet her lips, her eyes locked on his. Passion glazed her face, but her focus on him was laser sharp.

"Let go and feel," she said again, her words tight.

What else could he do?

His body was bombarded with sensations. Every nerve was awake and focused on one thing: satisfaction.

Their eyes locked, Phillip slid into her again.

And out.

Feelings, those damned emotions he'd always hated, washed over him as if her words had called them up.

To avoid them, he focused on his body.

On the sensations.

He slipped his hand between them, flicking that tiny bud between her thighs.

Frankie exploded.

Her body gripped his, her cries sending him crashing over himself.

Holy hell.

His mind too blown to be of any use, he tried to take stock of his body. The orgasm had been so intense even his toes were tingling. His heart was still pounding, pulse racing. The echo of Frankie's cries rang in his ears. He'd never felt anything like that before.

The desperate need clawing at him for more could be a potential issue, but he told himself he had enough command still to keep it under control.

Didn't he?

Breathless, numb, he shifted to take his weight off her, but she wouldn't let go.

"Not yet," she murmured faintly. "Stay for just a little longer."

Stay.

The temptation was overpowering.

For a second, Phillip relaxed against her again, the bulk of his weight on his elbows. Eyes closed, he rested his forehead against hers and tried to take it all in.

But he couldn't find any parameters for what he was feeling that would make sense.

He'd fought in the war. He'd served in combat, parachuted from planes, faced crazed terrorists and been held captive by a sadistic son of a bitch with a needle fetish.

But he'd never been scared.

The thought of staying, though? Of wanting someone enough to believe in possibilities? Of caring about something other than his career?

That filled him with terror.

All of a sudden, he felt as if the walls had slammed in around him, trapping him in the dark.

He had to get the hell out of there.

Phillip pulled away, a little slower this time. He saw Frankie pout but didn't stop. He got to his feet, frowning when his head did a fast spin. Too much alcohol, not enough food and intense physical exertion, he assessed.

That was why he was thinking crazy thoughts, he realized. Relief washed away the unfamiliar and unwelcome feeling of fear.

It wasn't some mythical emotion.

He was just slightly impaired.

Nothing to worry about.

And since it wasn't…

His gaze roamed Frankie's body as she lay there, one arm thrown over her eyes and a very big, very satisfied smile on her face.

His ego swelled a little knowing he'd put that smile there.

And now that he was sure he wasn't delusional, entertaining the idea of emotions that didn't exist, he could do it all over again. His eyes shifted to her full breasts, down the gentle indention of her waist to the full curve of her hips.

He wanted more.

And tonight, he was letting himself take more.

"Come on," he said, lifting her into his arms instead of waiting for her to get up. He made sure to grab the second condom, too.

"Where are we going?" she asked, her words muffled because she was scattering wet kisses over his chest, even as her hands locked behind his neck.

"Shower."

"Ooh, water sex," she exclaimed, laughing.

Filled with a warmth, a lightness he was attributing to the champagne they'd drank earlier, Phillip grinned.

"I'm a SEAL. I'm damned good in the water," he assured her, shifting her weight so he could start the shower. Not waiting for the water to warm up, he stepped right in, Frankie still nestled against his chest.

She squealed, burrowing into him to hide her face from the chilly spray.

Phillip laughed, delighting in her.

In the honesty of her reactions.

In the sweetness of her touch.

In the sexiness of her mouth.

In how he felt with her.

Free.

Swallowing hard, shoving aside the images trying to creep their way into this precious escape, Phillip pressed Frankie up against the shower wall. His mouth took hers, his hands sliding over her wet flesh.

His body, satisfied only a minute ago, demanded more.

His soul, at peace for the first time in months, demanded the same.

"Again already?" she gasped.

"I told you. I'm a SEAL. I'm damned good in water," he said, just before plunging into her.

Even as he drove, deep and hard, for both of their pleasure, the logical voice in the back of his head was glad she only had two condoms.

Not because he couldn't physically do this all night long. The way Frankie made him feel? He was pretty sure he could go for a week or two. Or forever.

So two was good.

Two set limit.

Frankie's body gripped his and her climax echoed in the stall as water pounded around them.

Phillip let go of all thoughts of forever, or of limits.

He let go of everything.

And for the first time in his life, as his orgasm swept over him, he simply felt.

FRANKIE DIDN'T KNOW how long she'd lain there, her mind in a race against her jumbled emotions.

After he'd proved that he could hold his own with any water god, Phillip had wrapped her in a towel and carried her to the bed. She'd almost come again when he'd gently dried the water from every inch of her body.

He'd followed that up by toasting her with the champagne a few dozen times.

And then he'd blown her mind.

Instead of initiating any form of sex, he'd climbed in beside her, wrapped her in his arms and simply, silently, cuddled her.

She was terrified.

She tried to count her breaths to calm herself, but every time she did, she started hyperventilating.

So she counted Phillip's breaths instead. In and out, in and out, until they deepened, slowed. Until he was asleep.

She relaxed then, but just a tiny bit.

Now, instead of his breath, she counted all of the stupid things she'd done tonight instead.

One, she'd totally forgotten her goal—to live out her fantasy. Actually, she'd forgotten everything. Fantasy, reason, logic, her own name.

Stupid.

Two, she'd gotten emotionally involved. She knew better. Phillip Banks was an incredible fantasy, but he wasn't her kind of guy. Or more to the point, she wasn't his kind of girl. She didn't do fancy; she wasn't upscale. The only time she'd been to a country club was when she and her friends had hopped the fence to chase an escaped cat.

Stupid, stupid, stupid.

Three, instead of focusing on the sensations, letting the sexual nirvana fill her creative well, all she'd been able to do about was think about him. Worry about him. All of her focus had been on trying to heal that hurt in his eyes.

Crazy.

One more round of mind-blowing sex and she'd have handed him her heart, offered to give up her dreams and, worse, begged him to call her sometime.

None of which he wanted.

Nor did she, dammit. No matter what she felt like right now.

Ever so carefully, not even breathing in case it woke

him, Frankie slipped out from under Phillip's arm and rolled off the bed.

Once on her feet, she froze, staring at him to make sure he was still asleep.

Then slowly, an inch at a time to avoid jangling any of the metal disks, she pulled her dress on. Her eyes never left Phillip's sleeping form as she felt around in the dark for her shoes. She checked the hidden zippered pocket, assuring herself that her key card was still there.

She needed to leave. Now, before he woke up.

But she couldn't bring herself to.

Knowing she was taking a huge risk, she tiptoed on bare feet to the edge of the bed. Just to look at him one last time. Even in sleep, he didn't look peaceful.

He looked like a warrior, reliving battles in his dreams.

Her heart ached, curiosity screaming to know what had hurt him so badly.

She told herself it didn't matter.

He would never tell her.

Besides, she didn't do rescues.

Especially not ones that would break her heart.

Moisture, salty and warm, slipped into the corner of her mouth as she stared down at him.

She wiped her hand over her cheek, realizing it was covered in tears.

She had to get out of there.

With one last look, she reached out as if to touch his cheek, but didn't let herself get that close. Instead, she forced herself to leave. Frankie opened the heavy door carefully, wincing as light from the corridor slanted into the room, temporarily blinding her.

Blinking against it and the tears still burning her eyes, she glanced back once, then carefully closed the door behind her.

Her shoes dangling from her fingers, Frankie leaned

her back against it and closed her eyes. She took a deep breath through her nose.

Phillip had been right.

This had been crazy.

The only saving grace was the fact that she was sure she'd never see him again.

And maybe, eventually, she'd convince herself that was a good thing.

4

A VICIOUS POUNDING dragged Phillip from the sleep of the dead.

His head throbbed, nausea churned in his gut and his eyes felt as if someone had sandblasted them before adding a coating of gasoline.

Holy crap, was this what a hangover felt like?

Phillip pressed the tips of his fingers against his closed eyes, hoping if he pushed hard enough the burning would fade. Or maybe his eyeballs would just pop on out. Whatever worked.

The pounding didn't stop.

It wasn't until he groaned that he realized it wasn't inside his head.

The door. Someone was knocking.

He peeled his eyelid open, sure he could hear a layer tearing off his eyeball, and squinted.

Hotel room?

Damn.

Las Vegas. Lara's wedding. Horrible dancing, noise and...

He flew from the bed, dragging the sheet with him.

"Frankie?" he asked, yanking the door open.

"Sir?"

Phillip squinted, his teeth clenched against the pain. Instead of a cute redhead with sexy freckles, a dark cloud stood in his doorway.

"Lane?" he muttered, pressing his fingers against his lids.

Shit.

Why was the petty officer here? They were still off duty, weren't they? Hadn't it only been one night? And if he was at the door, where had Frankie gone? Phillip turned back to the room, searching for her.

"We were all meeting for breakfast before heading for the airport," Lane reminded him. "You missed breakfast so I came to see if you'd changed your plans."

Breakfast?

Phillip squinted across the room, realizing the heavy drapes were closed tight.

It was morning?

He strode over, shoved the covers aside.

Nobody was there.

Damn.

He didn't bother looking in the bathroom. He knew she was gone.

"Hell." He sighed, dropping to the bed.

"Sir? You okay?"

"I think I slept with Frankie," he muttered.

"Whoa." The other man grimaced, holding up one hand in protest. "Is this the type of confession you really want to share? I'm not judging, man, but you've never been the bare-it-all kind of guy before. I hate to see you say something you'll regret more than…" Lane coughed uncomfortably. "Well, more than whatever you did here already."

"What?" His head in his hands, Phillip pressed his fingers against the sledgehammer pounding in his temples. Lane's words finally filtered through the pain and remnants of the vile cocktail his system had made of scotch and champagne. He groaned. "No."

"Beg pardon?"

Phillip risked spilling the contents of his stomach and lifted his head. "Frankie is a woman."

"Yeah? Cool, I guess." Lane shoved his hands in the front pocket of his jeans, looking as if he'd rather be anywhere but there. In perfect accord, Phillip shifted his gaze to the bedside clock.

How long had she been gone? How had he missed her leaving? He was a military specialist, highly trained in covert ops. And he'd slept through his one-night stand's walk of shame.

"Sir, are you okay?"

Lane's calling him "sir" wasn't a form of respect, or in deference to Phillip's rank. Nope, he frowned. That was his call sign. He'd always been a little amused by it in the past. He didn't mind being thought of as uptight and by the book. He was ambitious enough to want to—to plan to— climb to the rank of admiral, so just generally thought of it as his due. He'd been raised to command and expect power.

But today, when he felt so far from commanding or powerful, the name grated.

"You are whiter than those sheets," Lane noted. The guy didn't sound panicked or worried. He didn't move from his position by the door. But Phillip knew he was on full alert.

"Headache," Phillip muttered, dismissing the gut-clenching migraine. He needed meds fast, or this sucker was going to put him down.

"I'll meet you in the lobby in ten," he said, dismissing the petty officer without a glance. Partially because the guy was standing directly in a pool of sunshine and Phillip was pretty sure looking directly at the bright light would make his eyeballs explode. But mostly because he needed all of his focus, his entire concentration, to put one foot in front of the other.

He made it to the bathroom, grabbed a bottle of aspirin out of his toiletry bag, and dry-swallowed two pills. A steaming shower, a hundred push-ups and three bottles of water from the minifridge later and he felt like he'd live.

He glanced at the bed and winced.

He didn't do one-night stands.

He didn't have sex with strange women.

And he certainly didn't fall in love after seven hours. Hell, he didn't even believe in love, so falling was pure impossibility.

Wasn't it?

Phillip felt as though he was losing control. Everything was spinning out of bounds, even his own thoughts.

He wanted to know what the hell was wrong with him.

But he wasn't going to figure it out now.

He'd told Lane ten minutes, and he was never late.

Well, almost never. There was the notable exception of when he'd been captured by a sadistic drug kingpin with an unhealthy interest in infiltrating the Navy SEALs through torture and intimidation.

Shoving the memories aside along with the nagging pain still pounding at his head, Phillip grabbed his few belongings, tossed them in his bag and headed for the door.

His hand on the knob, he glanced at the bed again.

The image of Frankie's body spread beneath him filled his mind. The memory of her touch, of how it had felt to lose himself in her bombarded him.

He shook his head, hoping the pain would dislodge the thoughts. The sooner he put Las Vegas and last night behind him, the better. He wasn't worried about the memories. He'd just shove them in that same locked part of his mind where he kept all thoughts of his days as Valdero's guest.

FRANKIE SAT IN her studio, as she'd dubbed the third bedroom in her grandmother's cute little house, and tried not to scream. In her fist, she clenched the hideously lumpy mangled silver that had started out as a necklace.

What had happened?

Where were all the colors, the brilliant images and all that amazing creative juju?

She'd been sure she had it when she'd tiptoed out of Phillip's room. She'd had trouble sitting still on the plane ride home, she was so excited to get her hands on her tools. All it would take were a few pieces, maybe a dozen, to reestablish herself. A month or so to build up an inventory, maybe prep for a show.

By the time she'd unpacked her suitcase, she'd been able to see it all clearly. Her rise from the ashes, a celebrated return to glory. She'd have a stylish new condo by spring, be traveling around the country from gallery showings to high-end buyer meetings. Her pieces would be featured on television, in *Vogue,* maybe even in a movie or two.

And then she'd walked into her studio, smiling so big her cheeks hurt, and started to create.

Crap.

Frankie opened her fist to glare at the dull, unevenly linked spheres.

Every other thing she made was pure crap.

She knew she should be grateful that it wasn't every single thing. She was doing fine with simple pieces, reproductions of her earlier works.

But she was an artist. Not an assembly line.

And an artist created new pieces, dammit.

Ready to scream, she threw the failed necklace on the table, the force sending the silver bouncing to the floor. Frankie got to her feet, tossing aside her apron since its weight only slowed down her pacing.

What was she going to do?

She glanced at the ornaments ready for packaging, each exactly the same except for the name and date etched and echoed in gemstones.

Christmas was in a little more than a month.

What was she going to do after that? Make Valentine's ornaments? Fancy hangings to commemorate weddings and babies?

Frankie shoved her fingers into her hair, tugging to relieve the pressure.

How could any of that be considered creative? It couldn't. It just couldn't.

What had gone wrong?

After that night with Phillip, she'd felt the creative energy.

She'd seen so many pieces in her head, uniquely beautiful, each one in her signature quirky style.

After months of seeing nothing, it had been amazing. Like her birthday, five Christmases, graduation and incredible sex all rolled into one.

Incredible sex…

Heat washed over her, images flashing through her mind. Memories of Phillip, gloriously naked and poised over her body. Memories of that night, the orgasms—oh, the orgasms. So mind-blowing, so delicious.

She took a deep breath, her thighs trembling. She closed her eyes as heat coiled inside her, low and tight. Colors, images, designs flashed. So close. So, so close.

Maybe she could draw them. If she could get the images from her imagination onto paper, maybe—

"Frankie, the mail is here."

Frankie bit back the curses that wanted to tumble off her lips. She'd been so close. It was like being caught reading a naughty magazine just when you got to the good part.

But a girl didn't snap at her grandma, no matter how

delicious that good part might have been. Instead, Frankie plastered on her brightest smile and turned to the door.

"Thanks, Nana," she said, walking over to take the stack of envelopes. "I thought you were going to be at the seniors' center this morning."

Looking a good ten years younger than her sixty-five, Josephine O'Brian stood a foot taller and a half foot wider than the granddaughter she'd raised since Frankie's fourteenth birthday when a car accident had taken both Josephine's daughter and son-in-law.

"I was at the seniors' center for a while. But with Millicent and Olivia both on another cruise, it wasn't much fun."

"What about Deidre?" Frankie asked, referring to the fourth woman in her grandmother's close-knit group of friends.

"Off to her sister's for a couple of weeks."

Nana frowned and started to tidy the studio. Frankie had given up asking her not to. Apparently, the housekeeping urge was too deeply ingrained to ignore.

That, or she was bored. Nana was the only one of her friends not yet retired. While the others traveled and visited, she stayed faithful to her post at the Bankses' house. Since the elder Bankses had died almost three years back, she'd started taking short trips, long weekends. A year ago, Frankie had tried to convince her to actually retire, but Nana refused, saying the estate still needed her.

It was that loyalty, her devotion and her forty-plus years of service that had netted Josephine O'Brian a place in the Bankses' will. As long as a Banks owned the estate and Mrs. O'Brian was the housekeeper, she could live rent-free in the housekeeper's quarters at the back of the estate.

Sometimes Frankie wondered if part of the reason Nana wouldn't retire was because she had to look out for her flaky granddaughter.

Guilt, misery and frustration settled in Frankie's gut.

Despite the failure of her business, Nana insisted that her granddaughter continue designing. Five months ago, Frankie had started looking for a real job, something that would provide a regular income. Her grandmother had pitched a fit to end all fits, giving Frankie a solid understanding of where she'd gotten her temper.

Oh, what a lecture it had been. Nana had included everything from honoring one's gifts to disrespecting her elders. She'd thrown in a reminder of how proud Frankie's parents had been of her art and their hopes that she would make a living from it and wound it all up in a nice, guilty bow with a declaration of how important it was to her that Frankie revive her jewelry career.

So Frankie had done the only thing she could.

She'd moved in with her grandmother, taking advantage of the rent-free situation to pay down her debts while trying to recover her creative mojo.

To assuage some of her guilt over Nana not retiring yet, Frankie suggested, "Why don't you follow Deidre's lead? Go spend a few days with Aunt Isabelle and the cousins. I can take care of things here."

"Oh, no. I can't do that. Darling, I have work to do. The holidays are coming and the Banks house must be prepared."

Frankie opened her mouth to point out that nobody lived at the Banks house, so the only preparation necessary was making sure the place was clean and secure.

But her grandmother loved the holidays, the muss and fuss. She saw it as her duty to ensure that the house was prepared, just in case the family wanted to celebrate. The fact that Phillip had visited maybe twice since his parents' death and Lara only once in eight whole years didn't matter.

Josephine O'Brian never shirked her duties.

"How about dinner instead, then?" Frankie tucked her

arm through her grandmother's to lead her out of the room. Both because she was hungry, and because if Nana tidied any more she'd never be able to find anything.

"I always loved holidays at the Banks house," Nana said, wrapping her arm around her granddaughter's waist and giving her an affectionate squeeze. "Nobody did fancy like Ellen Banks. Remember the year the house was written up in that style magazine? People flocked to the house for months afterward, all wanting to say they'd been there. That was the only year she allowed the decorations to remain up for the New Year's festivities."

"Even the tree? How did she keep it alive?" Frankie wondered, knowing had to have been well over a month old since Nana always oversaw the decorating the weekend after Thanksgiving.

"Mrs. Banks had a new tree brought in." Nana chuckled. "Had us photograph the old one from all angles, strip it bare, then redecorate the fresh one in the wee hours of the night."

"Did the kids realize their tree had been redecorated?" Frankie asked with a laugh. Her smile faded as she imagined Phillip in front of a Christmas tree, his hair longer then and mussed from sleep. She'd bet her best soldering iron that he'd been adorable.

"The children weren't involved in the decorating," Nana said. Her tone was still proper, as it always was when she referred to her employers. But Frankie could hear something underneath. Sadness or disapproval—it was so faint she couldn't tell.

The image in Frankie's head changed. Now instead of a mussed and adorable younger Phillip, he was sadly looking at a fancily decorated tree from behind red velvet ropes. Those poor kids.

"That was one of the last holidays Lara spent at home,"

Frankie mused. "If I remember correctly, there were a lot of ugly fights leading up to that photo spread."

"Tut, Francesca," Nana chided as they stepped into the tidy kitchen. "Gossip is an ugly thing, and not something allowed on this estate."

"But gossip is the best source of news there is," Frankie countered with a teasing smile.

"You've always been full of sass, you have," Nana said. "Now, read your mail while I start the pasta, then you can make a salad."

Frankie flipped through the mail still in her hand.

Bill, bill, bill and, yes, another bill.

Frankie's shoulders sank so low she was surprised they weren't rubbing her hips. Looked as if she'd better call a few stores, see if they'd like to carry a display of her ornaments.

Or she could create a couple of stunningly awesome pieces of jewelry just in time for the holidays and rescue her career.

She gave a scoffing laugh under her breath.

She'd had her magical night; it was supposed to have fixed everything.

She bit her lip, fanning her thumb over the envelopes.

It had been a magical night. One she'd give anything to repeat. A few thousand times, even. Sooner or later, that kind of incredible sex had to break this block. Not just poke a few holes in it, but destroy it.

Frankie tapped the envelopes against her mouth, wondering what the chances were of getting her hands on that sexy SEAL again. Slim or none, most likely.

It was just as well. She remembered the depth of emotions that night had tapped. She'd never felt so much, so fast. Worry and lust had tangled together with a need to heal whatever had put that tortured look in Phillip's eyes, and something else.

Something crazy.

If it had been anyone else, she'd have said it was infatuation. The kind that led to even crazier things.

Like love.

A few more of those thousand times she'd been fantasizing about? She might do something seriously stupid and start thinking she was in love with the guy. She might believe there was a chance that they could have something that went beyond hot sex.

Decorated Navy SEAL, scion of the Banks family, the properest of the proper…and her?

As if.

Frankie almost snorted, and then she remembered how perfectly their bodies had fit together.

"Francesca? Start the salad, please."

Frankie startled, and the mail she'd been holding hit the floor. Her cheeks warmed. She had to stop thinking about that night. From now on, all thoughts of Phillip and sex were off-limits. Especially around her grandmother.

"Yes, Nana," she said, getting to work on the only part of the meal Nana deemed her skilled enough to prepare. The salad.

As she tore pieces of lettuce, she tried to find her optimism.

Sure, her career was a mess. But she'd get her creative mojo back, one way or another. She'd tried focusing on Phillip, on the sexual energy of her fantasies and then on her memories, but that hadn't worked, so she had to put him completely out of her head. Stop wasting energy on fantasies and funnel it all into her art.

She'd rebuild her career.

She'd get her artistic mojo back.

And she'd recover financially, so her grandmother could retire and enjoy her time with her friends.

Frankie started imagining what it would be like to be back on top.

On top of Phillip, perhaps.

His body hard and ready beneath hers. His eyes watching as she rode them both to screaming ecstasy.

Melting a little inside, Frankie gave up.

He was her fantasy guy.

She'd never get rid of him.

"LIEUTENANT BANKS."

Phillip stood at attention, waiting for the admiral to take the seat behind his desk.

It had been two weeks since Phillip's return to base, and he'd spent every one of those fourteen days waiting for this moment. Just as he'd spent every day of the previous two months hoping for it.

The retaliation mission.

It was time.

A chance to prove himself.

After this mission, he'd be back to normal.

Life would be back on track, his reputation as a topnotch SEAL restored. And the headaches, the crazy surges of emotion, the bizarre self-doubt, they'd all be gone.

About damned time.

Phillip hadn't expected the assignment to be handed down from the admiral himself. Nor would he expect to be the one getting the initial briefing. That should fall to Landon as the team leader. But who was he to question protocol? That he was the one standing here could mean good things.

For his career.

For the mission.

For revenge.

Phillip stiffened, shoving that last thought as deep into the far recesses of his brain as possible. He knew the admiral couldn't read his thoughts. He also knew most men, even some he served with, would consider the thought of taking vengeance on a man like Valdero fully justifiable.

But not the admiral.

He ground his teeth together, as if through pressure alone he could convince himself that it was.

Then the admiral cleared his throat, commanding Phillip's complete attention.

"The Navy doesn't take lightly to one of their own being detained, Lieutenant," Admiral Donovan said, folding his hands together precisely in the center of his desk blotter and giving Phillip an intense look.

"No, sir."

"Intelligence has determined the leak that led to your capture and taken care of it."

Phillip clenched his teeth, but didn't ask where the leak had been, if it was internal or external. That information was classified, and well above his security clearance. He had his own suspicions, and had reported them during debriefing. But he hadn't mentioned them again. He'd had plenty of time to think about it, to obsess over every second of that mission, to analyze every word Valdero had uttered.

Yeah. He had his suspicions. And he'd confirm them personally as soon as he returned to Guatemala.

And when he did, he'd deal with it his way.

"Normally this order would come down from your commanding officer, but in light of everything, I am choosing to issue it personally."

The admiral had been one of Phillip's instructors at Annapolis years ago. He'd known his grandfather and had taken a personal interest in Phillip's career.

Phillip didn't believe in favors, especially those that touched on nepotism. He'd earned his stars.

Anticipation, the kind he felt just before a mission,

surged through his system. Phillip's chin came up a fraction, triumph settling in his belly.

This was it.

The order to lead the mission that would take down that sadistic son of a bitch, Valdero, code name Candy Man.

The admiral stood, cleared his throat and stared directly at Phillip.

"Effective immediately, you're being transferred to the United States Naval Academy, Annapolis."

There was a buzzing in his ears, that now-familiar-but-once-unheard-of fury pounding at his temples.

"Transferred?" Phillip repeated, certain the man had misspoken.

"Temporarily." The admiral flipped open a file, but didn't take his eyes away from Phillip's. "You're one of the foremost experts on security measures. We'd like you to head a new security program being launched at the training center in Annapolis. Monday at oh-eight-hundred, you'll report to the Naval Academy for further instructions."

He was off the mission?

Off the mission, and the base?

To talk about security to a bunch of college kids?

Bracing against the avalanche of rage pouring through him, Phillip tried to rein it in. Tried to grab hold of his emotions. It was as if the serene flow that had been his carefully planned life had been rerouted to a freaking waterfall. Totally out of control and impossible to navigate.

"For how long, sir?" he asked between tightly clenched teeth.

"First of the year."

Until the training and the mission were over, Phillip realized. They wanted him out of the way. And apparently off the team wasn't enough; they were sending him to the other side of the country.

He clenched his fists, channeling all of the anger, all the frustration into his fingers and holding it there, tight.

He didn't say a word until he was sure he was in command again.

"With all due respect, sir, I'm the best person to lead that mission." Dammit, he was. He'd been held captive inside that compound for three days. He'd looked Valdero in the eyes while the sick bastard had used his body as a pincushion, trying to extract naval intelligence. He'd survived, dammit. He deserved this mission.

"Negative."

Phillip had spent his entire life respecting the chain of authority. His father was a man who demanded it. His career with the Navy required it. His personality insisted upon it.

He wasn't an emotional man. Emotions led to drama, and drama was a waste of energy and a loss of control. Two things he'd always refused to allow.

But that refusal didn't mean jack when faced with the waves of anger—righteous anger, dammit—pounding through his system. The rage that had been bubbling and churning since Guatemala bubbled and boiled, ready to spew.

Thankfully, before it overtook his tenuous control, there was a knock on the door.

At the admiral's command, another officer entered.

Phillip automatically saluted.

"Lieutenant, this is Lieutenant Commander Donovan."

Lieutenant Commander Mitch Donovan, a legend among legends.

A man who, until this moment, Phillip had admired. Whose career he'd wanted to emulate.

Phillip's hands, clasped behind his back, clenched into fists.

Jaw tight, he eyed the man there to take his place. The

admiral's grandson, no less. He didn't need to hear the rest of the admiral's words to know Donovan had been brought in to lead the mission to capture Valdero.

If they'd brought Donovan in, the mission was bigger than before.

"Sir, I request permission to serve with my team," Phillip tried again.

"Negative." The admiral came around his desk, stopping a foot in front of Phillip and giving him a penetrating stare. "Unless you'd like to add something else to your debriefing that'd be useful to your team, you can stand down."

Phillip's jaw worked as he struggled to rein in his anger until he was sure he wouldn't explode.

His gaze cut to Donovan, expecting to see the same rigid dismissal in his eyes as the admiral's. Instead, he saw understanding. A hint of sympathy. And a promise. The job would be done. And it would be done right.

Rather than reassuring him, however, it made Phillip all the angrier.

He had to get out of there.

"Lieutenant, you have your orders," the admiral said. "Dismissed."

It wasn't the dismissal that made Phillip do an about-face and walk out.

It was the uncontrollable fury pounding in his temples.

And the barrage of unfamiliar doubts.

About his abilities.

About his career.

About his entire life.

5

PHILLIP PARKED HIS rental vehicle in the wide circular driveway of his childhood home and looked around.

Not out of nostalgia. He didn't have any happy memories of growing up here. It was simply the responsible
thing to do, he thought, as he inspected the large fountain
in the center of the driveway and the emerald expanse of
lawn. Not visible from the driveway, but surely in just
as pristine condition, were the tennis courts, swimming
pool and servants' quarters behind the rose hedge at the
far end of the lawn.

It looked the same.

Phillip frowned.

It looked *exactly* the same.

He didn't know why that surprised him.

Change was a dirty word in the Banks family.

Something he'd accepted without question his entire
life.

So why did it grate like fingernails on a chalkboard
right now?

He eyed the steps leading to the ornate oak door, their
curved angles flanked by two huge marble pillars. Each
pillar stood in a sea of pale pink roses. Not red, not dark
pink. Ellen Banks hadn't believed in strong statements.

It didn't matter that she'd been gone two years and eight months; her preferences still ruled all.

Leaving the car in the driveway, he headed for the steps. Then stopped in his tracks and glanced over his shoulder. The driveway was for guests. Family cars belonged in the garage.

Unlike Lara, he'd never wanted to buck tradition or thumb his nose at the rules. Leaving the car there was simply practical.

His luggage and equipment were in there.

There was no point bringing his things inside until he knew the house was prepared. Besides, he hadn't decided yet if he was staying here or finding housing at Lincoln Military.

Still, he had to force himself up those stairs, every step that he took bringing echoes of past lectures to mind. Since it was a change from the myriad of other unwelcome thoughts he'd been entertaining lately, he let them echo away as he opened the door.

The foyer was waxed and polished, a vase of frilly blooms on the sideboard and the chandelier overhead gleaming.

Phillip shivered in spite of his leather jacket.

The chill had nothing to do with the cool November morning.

Warmth was pretty much forbidden here.

As was laughter, unless it was politely restrained.

Dreams, unless they'd been vetted and approved.

Goals were good, though. Those were handed out from the head of the table every night at dinner and reviewed every Sunday. Progress was expected, failings not tolerated.

Was it any surprise that Lara had bolted?

Phillip stepped into the parlor, as his mother had called

the front living room. He shoved his hands into his pockets, glaring at the portrait over the fireplace.

The esteemed Banks family, in all their glory.

The matriarch, perfectly coifed in Chanel and pearls,
was seated on a throne-like chair next to her husband.
Phillip narrowed his eyes, surprised to realize how much
he looked like his father. He hadn't at sixteen when the
portrait had been painted. The similarities then had been
between him and Lara, who everyone had said looked like
their mother before her second, third and fourth facelifts.

Something he was sure Lara hadn't appreciated.

Phillip's lips quirked at the boredom in his sister's eyes.
Their parents had been able to force her to smile politely,
but Lara had always found a way to make her dissatisfac-
tion known.

Unlike her, he'd never questioned his place in this house.

In his family.

His parents had been proud.

They wouldn't be now. His father would rage over Phillip.

And his mother?

Phillip snorted.

She'd be pissed about his scars. He held his hands out,
fingers wide, to inspect the crosshatch of white lines
scored from knuckle to wrist. Unlike the scars on his back
and chest, these were always visible, impossible to ignore.

Unlike his father, she wouldn't care that they were physical proof of his failure.

She'd simply be horrified because they were ugly.

God, what did he come from? And why did he suddenly
care? Soul-searching wasn't something he typically en-
gaged in. Yet lately, it had become second nature.

Frowning, Phillip squared his shoulders, and as he
did with anything that didn't fit his plans, he shoved the
thought out of his head.

And, as if it had been waiting for the all-clear, an image rushed in.

The image of Frankie, naked and deliciously tempting.

The sound of her cries as she exploded beneath him.

The feel of her body, milking every last drop of pleasure from his.

Phillip blew out a breath and shook his head, trying to dislodge that image, too. It didn't budge as easily as the frustration and irritation that had become his everyday companions.

Then again, fantasies of Frankie had become his buffer against insomnia and nightmares and were fast replacing pain meds in staving off those damned migraines.

But none of those were an issue now.

Now it was time to get on with things. And get something to eat. He headed toward the back of the house.

"Mrs. O'Brian?" he called out, stepping into the kitchen. "I'm home."

"Indeed you are." Looking the same as she had every day of his life, Mrs. O'Brian came around the stove, wiped her hands on her apron and held them out to welcome him. Her hands were as soft as the dough she'd been kneading. Brown eyes sparkled behind her wire-rimmed glasses, and her white hair was braided to wrap around her head like a crown. Fitting. His mother had ruled the front of the house, but Mrs. O'Brian had ruled the kitchen and beyond.

"Don't you look wonderful," she exclaimed, squeezing his hands. "Much better than your last visit."

Phillip's polite smile didn't shift, nor did he correct her. The last time he'd been back was for his parents' memorial service. He'd been whole then. Of sound mind and undamaged body.

"I hope you have something for me to eat," Phillip said, easily shifting the subject as he released her fingers and stepped back.

"Roast-beef sandwiches, fresh-cut fries and apple pie for dessert?" she offered, her smile twinkling. "Your favorite lunchtime fare. Dinner will be more robust, of course."

Robust? Base food had nothing on Mrs. O'Brian's cooking. Phillip made a mental note to arrange to use the academy gym. Might as well, since he'd be there daily. Teaching. Or being punished. They were pretty much the same thing.

"The house looks great, Mrs. O'Brian," he told her, glancing over her shoulder. The pool sparkled inside a glass-enclosed room, the patio furniture gleamed and the patio drapes fluttered in the autumn breeze. "You didn't have to go to all this trouble, though."

"It was no trouble, Mr. Phillip. My granddaughter helped out."

Phillip nodded, vaguely remembering Mrs. O'Brian's various granddaughters visiting her from time to time.

"Still, I don't want to put you out," he said, preparing to tell her he wouldn't be staying.

"Trouble? Oh, no, this is a pleasure. I miss having people here, someone to take care of. Having you home, especially at the holidays, it's a special treat," she said. Her smile was so bright that Phillip couldn't bring himself to say anything that would dim it.

"Go on now, into the dining room," the older woman instructed, waving her hand to shoo him out of the kitchen.

"I can eat in here. I don't want you serving me," he refused.

"No eating in the kitchen," she said, in a familiar refrain. She turned, lifting an already prepared tray. "Here, you can take this into the dining room. I'll send your dessert in soon."

Phillip looked at the tray, wondering how she'd timed it so the fries were still hot.

Hungry, he figured he'd use this time to map out what

was definitely a questionable lesson plan. After all, lecturing about keeping his mouth shut while being tortured was barely enough to fill one lesson, and the admiral had mandated eight.

A half hour later, Phillip glared at the notes he'd sketched across a pad he'd found in the sideboard.

The only part of him that felt satisfied was his stomach. He wasn't a trainer. He didn't want to be. But an assignment was an assignment, and he couldn't afford another failure.

Phillip pressed his fingers to his closed eyelids, trying to massage away the stress before it climbed into headache territory.

Then his senses hit overload.

He lifted his head, looking around.

A delicious overload.

He smelled the apple pie a good five seconds before he saw the tray coming around the corner.

Phillip didn't miss a whole lot about this house—except Mrs. O'Brian's desserts.

He stood, ready to take the tray and thank her.

Then he saw the face behind the tray.

A roaring filled his ears.

Carefully preserved images bombarded him. His body reacted as strongly as it had that night a month ago. Need and desire he didn't want to feel, didn't know how to deal with, washed over him.

Still, he kept his expression blank as he inspected the bearer of his apple pie.

A gorgeous redhead, her hair pulled back but untamed. His eyes shifted, taking in her white poet-style blouse and slim jeans tucked into knee-high boots. Sassy, sexy and, oh, so tempting.

"Frankie?"

"Uh-oh." Eyes huge, Frankie looked horrified.

Since he knew she'd been every kind of sexually satisfied the last time he'd seen her, he didn't take her reaction personally.

Of course, she'd also snuck out of the hotel room in the middle of the night without so much as a word, a nudge or even a note.

He frowned.

Maybe it was personal.

No. Oh, no, no, no. Not Phillip. Not here.

She could have sworn Nana said Lara was here. Granted, she'd been in the middle of a meltdown when her nearly completed bracelet had melted under a too-hot torch.

But tantrum or not, she'd definitely have heard Phillip's name.

Wouldn't she have?

Frankie's stomach pitched into her toes. Her hands shook; the plate rattling on the tray. She forced her fingers to steady, knowing Nana would have a fit if she broke a plate.

"What are you doing here?" he asked quietly.

A dozen excuses, half of them lies, flew through Frankie's head. She didn't see how any of them would work, though. Any chance of keeping her identity secret was blown.

He looked so good.

So, so good.

And so proper. Phillip Banks, back in his natural setting.

Seeing him here flipped her fantasy guy from hot and sexy to completely off-limits.

She didn't like it. Not one bit.

"I didn't know you were here," she said, her words barely above a whisper.

"Who were you expecting?"

"Um, Lara?" she said, her voice shaky. She cleared her throat. "I thought she was visiting."

"Lara, who ran away from this house at sixteen and cut off all ties with her family? You thought she was going to follow up her honeymoon bliss by coming here?" He gave her a sardonic look, and then, clearly tired of waiting, got up to take the tray out of her hands.

"She visited a couple of months ago," Frankie muttered, feeling like an idiot. She'd helped clean the house yesterday. She'd even put flowers in Lara's old bedroom and cleared her calendar for the next few evenings in case Lara wanted to get together. She'd never thought it might be Phillip visiting.

She'd never let herself *think* he might visit.

But now that he had?

Her heart raced, her thoughts spinning just as fast. One night with him had sparked inspiration. Now that he was here…how much spark could they generate? Was it worth the trouble certain to go along with it?

Not sure, needing to buy a little time to think, Frankie took a deep breath, pulled back her shoulders and lifted her chin.

"How's the pie?" she asked, angling her body a little and giving him a flirtatious smile.

"Good. Fresh apples, right?"

What?

She looked at the pie, tilting her head to peer at the chunks of apple. Fresh? How would she know?

"Sure," she guessed, watching him dig into his pie as if seeing his Las Vegas one-night stand didn't faze him at all.

"So why are *you* here?" she asked, stepping closer. Close enough that the scent of his soap filled her senses. She leaned one hip against the table. She wanted to touch him, to slide her fingers along his cheek. To what? Offer comfort? He didn't look like he needed it anymore.

Phillip shrugged, scooping up another bite of pie, totally focused on his dessert. Not on her.

Frankie frowned.

She'd spent the past three weeks obsessed with the guy. Lying awake at night reliving that night in her imagination, sitting in her studio trying to turn those memories into art. He'd rocked her world, and what? She barely registered on his radar? Then she saw the look in his eyes.

Veiled interest, hot curiosity.

Oh, boy.

That look was all it took. Memories of that night surfaced in all their glory.

She wet her lips, her stomach tightening as his eyes followed the move. He didn't say anything, though. Just carefully cut his crust in two as if wanting to make his pie last as long as possible.

A habit he brought to other appetites as well, she remembered. The heat in her stomach uncoiled, spreading through her body.

Temptation spiraled through her system.

"Are you here for long?" she asked, ignoring that he hadn't answered her previous question yet.

"I've been assigned to the Naval Academy until the end of the year." His eyes narrowed as he glanced at the pad of paper next to his plate. "And you?"

"Me?"

"Why are you here and for how long?" Phillip asked, his smile polite, his expression making it clear he wasn't going to let her avoid the question any longer.

Frankie debated.

No matter what she told him, Nana would out her sooner or later. And while Phillip might be open to a little wild time with one of his sister's friends in Las Vegas, she somehow doubted he'd be nearly as interested in the housekeeper's granddaughter.

For a brief—very brief—second, Frankie wondered if there was time for one more round before he found out who she was.

But that would be wrong.

Good, but wrong.

Ashamed of herself for even considering it, she offered him her most charming smile and pulled out the chair next to his. With a quick glance to make sure her nana wasn't nearby, she slid onto the brocade-covered seat.

"I'm Frankie, just like I said," she told him with her brightest smile. She would try the seductive one again, since it had worked so well before, but she figured she'd be smarter to save that for when it had a chance of actually working.

"I didn't ask who you were," he reminded her, pressing his fork against the flakes of crust left on his plate. "I asked what you were doing here."

"I'm here bringing dessert." She tapped one finger on the edge of his plate and wiggled her brows. "Did you want more pie?"

"You work here?" he asked, pushing the plate away with one finger.

Frankie's smile slipped a little.

"Nope, I told you, I'm a silversmith."

"And you're a friend of Lara's?" Eyes narrowed, Phillip leaned back in his chair a little.

"Well, sort of a friend," she said honestly. "We never buddied up when she lived at home. You know Lara, she was totally into dance."

"And she's a couple years older than you," he observed, giving her a searching look over steepled fingers.

"A year and a half." Frankie nodded.

"You're not a dancer. You weren't in class with her. So how do you know her?"

"You say that like you have doubts about your sister having friends."

"Lara does tend to be a little on the prickly side." He tilted his head to the side. "But you were at her wedding, so I'm not doubting your claim."

"Well, then—"

"You still haven't told me why you're here."

Frankie wrinkled her nose.

It wasn't as if she was ashamed of her position in life. Or in the social pecking order, even.

She shifted her butt on the antique chair, suddenly very aware that the contents of the dining room alone were worth more than her entire family's assets.

And she was thinking there was a possibility they could repeat what they'd done in Las Vegas?

She bit her lip, her eyes searching Phillip's face. His expression was polite, just a hint of curiosity in his green eyes. Had she imagined the heat in his eyes a few minutes ago?

Because that look on his face wasn't the look of a man who was interested in reprising his sexual fling.

It was still better than the looks she'd seen plenty of times in this house over the years.

The master-to-servant look.

It'd never mattered to Mr. or Mrs. Banks that she wasn't actually one of their staff. Inferior was inferior after all.

She didn't want to see that look on Phillip's face.

Distant.

Cool.

As if they'd never licked each other's bodies, as if they'd never watched each other come alive with pleasure.

"Francesca, what on earth is taking you so long?"

Frankie dropped her face into her hands and bit back a cry.

Why, oh, why did her grandmother keep interrupting

her fantasies about Phillip? It was enough to ruin a girl's hopes for getting lucky.

Of course, now that she'd been outed, she probably didn't need to worry about that anymore.

Grimacing, she looked up in time to see Phillip's eyes widen, then narrow to inspect her face.

His gaze shifted behind her, then back.

Frankie sighed.

Yeah, getting lucky was definitely off the table.

"I'm just welcoming Phillip home, Nana," she said without looking around. "He ate that pie in two big bites."

"I figured he would, which is why I had another slice cut and waiting," Nana said, bustling into the room and setting a new plate in front of Phillip.

She gave his empty dishes a satisfied look, then arched a brow at her granddaughter as she stacked them on the tray.

"I'm glad you're keeping him company, Frankie. Phillip needs a friend while he's home."

Frankie's surprise quickly turned to delight at the idea of being Phillip's friend…his very, very good friend. Then she caught the look on his face. Her lips twitched at his shocked eyes and confused frown.

"You keep him company, but don't be a pest," Nana said, patting Frankie's shoulder before lifting the tray.

Frankie waited for the sound of her grandmother's footsteps to die away before settling her elbows on the table and leaning forward.

"You need a friend?" she asked, wriggling her eyebrows and giving him a naughty smile.

"Do you have a habit of being a pest?" he asked, looking politely curious again. How did he do that? Just tuck his emotions away and pretend they weren't there?

Frankie wondered if that look was a product of his upbringing or his SEAL training.

Whatever the reason, it was seriously intimidating.

"So...you were asking how I know Lara?" she asked, her tone bright.

"Mrs. O'Brian is your grandmother." He gave her a nod, acknowledging the fact. Then he pulled his second piece of pie closer and dug in. "She makes the best pie in the country."

"Have you tried all the pie in the country to compare?"

"Thirty-two of the fifty states."

"Just apple?" she asked, tapping the table next to his plate. "Or do you try every flavor, you know, in the name of comparison?"

"Apple, cherry, pumpkin." He forked up another bite, ate it, then nodded. "I haven't had her pumpkin in a long time, though. There's a café in Idaho that does amazing things with squash. Maybe you could ask her to make one this week."

"For comparison's sake?"

"Of course."

"Why don't you ask her yourself?"

"Me? I think the roof would cave in." Phillip gave a short laugh. "This is the house of restraint. Desserts were for holidays, and even then portions were minuscule. Like alcohol and other indulgences, a taste was all that was necessary."

What was it like to grow up that way? So used to following her emotions, to chasing sensations, Frankie barely understood the concept of moderation. Heck, her credit card bill and the snug waistband of her jeans were proof of that.

But to Phillip, it was second nature. Frankie wanted to reach out and pull him into her arms, to hug him close.

Bad idea.

She looked at her fingers, twisted together on the rich mahogany table, and wet her lips.

"So aren't you going to say anything?"

"What have I been doing for the past ten minutes?"

Frankie wasn't sure if he was joking or looking for clarification. His expression was so serious, so proper.

Her jaw tightened, resignation settling over her like a prickly blanket. She didn't understand him. Gone was the vulnerability, the need she'd seen in Vegas. He wasn't the cute, smart rich boy she'd crushed on in her teen years.

Suddenly, the differences between her fantasy Phillip and the real-life Phillip were glaringly obvious.

She could justify doing anything with the fantasy Phillip. Risking anything. The results were always worth it. The satisfaction, the fulfillment. The supercharged creative juices. The fantasy Phillip was the answer to all her problems. He thought she was amazing; he turned to her for comfort. Her fantasy Phillip, he needed her.

The real-life Phillip didn't need her. He didn't even understand her. He had total control over his emotions and was so far outside her world that they might as well have addresses on different planets.

Both Phillips were gorgeous.

Sexy.

Tempting.

But while the fantasy Phillip was one of the greatest enjoyments in her life, she didn't understand the real-life man. He was a stranger. An uptight, proper, closed stranger who had been raised on the opposite side of very clear class distinctions.

A wave of sadness washed over Frankie, her bottom lip trembling for a moment before she clenched her jaw. She hadn't felt this bad since she'd had a goodbye ceremony for her imaginary friend when she was nine.

Time to grow up again, she told herself.

Let go of the fantasy and accept that there was nothing, nothing *real,* between her and Phillip.

"Frankie?" he said, verbally nudging her back into the conversation.

"We haven't been talking," she decided, meeting his eyes. "We've been dancing."

His eyes went hot.

He gave her a long, considering look as he pushed his plate away.

"We've danced before. I promise you, this doesn't feel anything like dancing."

"You do remember," she blurted out.

His lips twitched. "Remember what?"

Just like that, Frankie's good intentions crumbled under her delight.

Oh, man.

She was so, so bad at restraint.

And even worse at denying herself anything she wanted.

And real life or fantasy, she definitely wanted Phillip Banks.

6

PHILLIP DIDN'T BELIEVE in things like divine intervention, heavenly gifts or special blessings.

But as he watched Frankie laugh, the light dancing in her dark eyes, he was pretty sure she was an angel.

She had to be.

Just watching her filled him with pleasure.

Not just sexual pleasure, although that was unquestionably there, pressing tight against his zipper.

Not emotional. At least he didn't think so. He didn't understand emotions. Until they'd exploded all over his life after his capture, he'd have sworn he barely had any.

He wasn't sure what this was he was feeling as he looked at Frankie, as her laugh drew a smile from him.

All he knew was it felt good.

"Remember what, my tush," Frankie challenged, leaning forward and giving his arm a playful swat. "You remember everything about that night. Admit it."

Phillip leaned back in his chair, tapping his fingers on the table while looking her over.

Her ponytail swept around her shoulder in a riot of curls that brushed the top of her breast. Her skin glowed, sprinkled with golden freckles. She was a vivid contrast to the cold room, the colder memories it held.

He couldn't resist her warmth.

"Hmm, remember," he mused, drawing out the words. "I'll admit I might have a vague recollection of dancing with a sexy redhead."

Her smile widened, and this time when she tapped her fingers against his arm it felt more like a caress. A simple touch, lasting only a second through the fabric of his shirt, and his body reacted instantly, desire strong and intense.

All of the fury, tension and frustration that had been dogging him shrank back into the shadows.

"Mmm, was it a good dance?" she asked, her fingers now tracing circular designs on the table next to his hand. She didn't touch. Just teased, hinted. Exciting him.

"Best dance I've ever had in Monaco," he said.

It wasn't easy to keep a straight face when Frankie gave a fake gasp, then shook her head at him.

"Las Vegas," she corrected primly.

"We drank brandy," he offered, moving his hand a little closer to hers.

"Champagne."

"Then we took the stairs down twenty flights."

"Elevator," she corrected, her fingers tracing the edge of his. Heat shot through him like an electric charge.

Phillip tried to focus on the game. But it was difficult. He was—or had been before Valdero—a master at focusing. He had become gifted in the art of tunnel vision. He could perform perfectly under any distraction.

But he wasn't used to playing.

And he was surprised to find he liked it.

"Twenty flights?" he asked quietly, concentrating on her face in order to block out the distractions.

"Um, I don't actually remember that," she admitted with a husky laugh, her fingers now skimming the back of his hand. Phillip didn't have a lot of experience in strip clubs—the closest he'd ever come was dragging a wounded ensign out of one after a brawl. But he was pretty sure he couldn't be more turned on if she'd climbed on top of him and offered him a lap dance.

Phillip's gaze shifted to her breasts, full and tempting under the flowing white cotton of her blouse.

Wrong. She could turn him on a whole lot more.

But that didn't negate how sexually charged he was already.

"Three flights," he said huskily. He cleared his throat and met the question in her eyes. "We kissed all the way down those three flights in the elevator."

"We did," she agreed, wetting her lips.

He wondered if she could taste him still.

Some nights he'd awake from a dead sleep with the taste of her on his tongue and his body hard and yearning.

"Then what happened?" she asked.

"We went to my room." He could see everything that happened after that. He vividly remembered every touch, every sound. Every taste. But he couldn't recap it. Not out loud.

He tore his gaze from Frankie's, glancing around the room. Stuffy and elegant, the family dining room was warmer than the formal dining room, but not by much.

He could just hear his mother lamenting her children's poor manners and improper behavior. Her chiding was easily drowned out by his father's lectures on success at all costs.

Phillip all but cringed.

This was definitely not the place he wanted to discuss sex, cravings or unforgettable nights.

Somewhere else, then?

He took a mental tour of the house in search of someplace he could take Frankie.

And came up blank.

He couldn't think of a single room in this damned house that would be suitable.

Which was telling, since he wasn't even sure what he'd do with her if he found the right place.

All he knew was that he wanted her. Wanted the peace, the mindlessness that night in Vegas had offered. He'd been dreaming of that night ever since it happened. It had become his talisman against the migraines, his hope for a decent night's sleep—sexy dreams notwithstanding.

He'd been satisfied with the memories. They worked.

But to do it again?

It wasn't often that life offered second chances.

Most people would say he was a fool if he didn't take this one.

Phillip frowned.

The house was a reflection of the Banks family. Of their priorities, their sensibilities, their values.

And he was a product of the same.

What was he doing lusting after a woman he barely knew?

Certain behaviors were understandable under certain circumstances. But this wasn't tawdry Las Vegas. It was the Banks house.

Phillip pressed one finger against his nose, right next to his right eye, where the headache was starting to take hold.

"You're disappearing," Frankie said.

He dropped his hand to his lap and frowned.

Her expression hadn't changed. But he could hear the disappointed resignation in her voice.

As if she'd expected him to do just that.

"I'm right here."

"Your body is, sure. But as fine as that body is, and as much as I'm enjoying the view, you're still not here. You drifted off somewhere," she observed with a little shrug that did amazing things with the fabric of her blouse. Slippery, sliding things.

Phillip had been in war. He'd successfully fought many battles, had distinguished himself on the field.

But he'd never felt a war such as the one going on inside him right now.

His gut clenched as he wondered if this was just more proof that he was struggling with his life. The Navy, his admiral, probably his own team doubted his abilities.

Maybe they were right.

"Why didn't you tell me who you were?" he asked Frankie, needing to avoid that ridiculous line of thinking.

"I did tell you," she said, fire lighting in those dark eyes, assuring him that she had a temper to match her hair. "I am Frankie Silvera. And I am a friend of your sister's."

"You omitted a few details, though. Why didn't you mention Mrs. O'Brian? Or that you lived in Annapolis? I thought you were a friend of Lara's from Reno."

"Does it matter?" She leaned back in her chair, arms crossed over her chest. One slender denim-clad leg crossed over the other had her foot tapping the air in time with her fingers drumming on her shoulder.

Phillip's lips twitched.

For a woman who apparently kept secrets, she was damned good at sending messages.

"If it doesn't matter, why wouldn't you tell me?"

She opened her mouth, looking as though she was going to breathe fire. Phillip leaned forward, excitement stirring inside him. Had he ever met anyone so alive? So passionate?

What would she do next?

Yell? Throw her arms in the air and curse? His body stirred. Maybe throw a plate? He'd never broken a dish in his life. That had to be why imagining her tossing one across the room was getting him hard.

Then she let out a long breath, her shoulders dropping, lips sinking into a pout.

"I didn't want you to know who I really was in case you remembered me," she said quietly.

His eyes were still on that full bottom lip, wondering what it would taste like if he leaned forward for a nibble. It took a second for what she'd said to sink in.

He shifted his gaze to her eyes, searching for the reason behind the shame there.

"Why would that matter?" he asked, truly baffled.

"I'm the housekeeper's granddaughter," she said, drawing the words out in an unspoken "duh." "You're, well, you. If you knew who I was, there's no way that night would have happened."

So she thought he was a snob. Insult surged through his system. He wasn't oblivious to his family's prejudices, but that didn't mean he shared them.

"That's not true." His brow creased as honesty forced him to admit, "I don't know that our choices that night were the best ones. But I do know that knowing who your grandmother was, who you really are, wouldn't have impacted my decision in the least."

"Right." Her smile stiff, Frankie stood, leaning across the table to take his dessert plate and fork.

Phillip's libido came to attention.

But she didn't throw the plate. She tidily set the fork on top of it and moved to leave.

His libido shrank in disappointment.

So did his stomach at the look on her face.

She was hurt.

Damn.

He couldn't stand it.

He could ignore his own wants, the clawing need he had to touch her. He could hide behind propriety and decorum, list the many reasons why a man dedicated to a military career shouldn't be fooling around with a woman who clearly deserved more.

He could even try to tell himself it was for their own good to ignore the passion sparking between them like an exposed electrical wire.

But he couldn't let her think he didn't want her—not because of something as antiquated as social standing.

"Frankie," he said, automatically using the same tone he would to order troops to halt.

She didn't halt, though.

She did slow down long enough to give him an eye roll over her shoulder.

He hurried forward, grabbing her arm just as she reached the doorway.

"Wait," he said, more softly this time. Turning her around, he trapped her between his body and the wall so she couldn't escape.

Her hiss sounded like water tossed on flames. Her eyes sparked as she fisted the plate and fork in her fingers like a weapon.

She was so damned sexy.

"It wouldn't have impacted my decision in the least," Phillip repeated adamantly.

Then he took her mouth.

For a brief moment, she froze.

Then he felt her deep inhalation against his mouth and she exploded, her mouth racing against his. He felt a dull *thunk* as the plate hit his back when she wrapped her arms around him.

She tasted so good.

He leaned into her body, her curves molding to his hard length.

She felt even better.

Filled with a level of desperation he hadn't felt since

Las Vegas when he'd last seen Frankie naked, Phillip lost himself in the kiss.

Her lips opened beneath his, her mouth welcoming his tongue. Passion stirred in him, rising hotter and higher with every sweep of his tongue. He wanted to drag her upstairs, kick open the door of his childhood bedroom, toss her on the rock-hard mattress and strip her bare.

He wanted to taste more than her mouth.

Frankie made that little sound, a mewling sort of sigh. The last time he'd heard her make that sound, he'd been inside her body watching her buck with pleasure.

His body clenched, need pounding through him with an intensity he'd never felt before.

It was all Phillip could do not to take her right there against his mother's silk-papered wall.

Frantically grasping for control before it slipped out of reach, he tore his mouth from hers and stepped away.

A kiss.

A simple kiss had his hands shaking.

This was crazy.

Completely inappropriate.

It took a deep breath, then another one, before Phillip was sure he wasn't going to reach for Frankie again.

Eyes huge, she watched him as if in a daze.

When she wet her swollen lips, he almost said to hell with it all and kissed her again.

If they'd been in Vegas, or anywhere else, he would have.

But as compelling as second chances, cravings and throbbing desire were, he was still a Banks.

This was Maryland, and the family estate.

Not Las Vegas.

At the very least, he had to buy her dinner first.

"What are you doing Friday evening?" he asked, mentally cringing at how lame the question sounded.

Frankie's lips moved as if she was silently repeating his words in order to understand them. The glaze of passion faded from her eyes as she frowned.

Head tilted to one side, she asked, "Why?"

"I'd like to take you to dinner."

"DINNER?"

Phillip wanted to take her out to dinner?

Seriously?

Frankie considered doing a little happy dance, right then and there. The only thing that stopped her was the fact that she knew she'd look ridiculous.

That, and the chance that she had misunderstood. She hated getting her hopes up, since the inevitable fall always hurt so badly.

"Dinner. The meal at the end of the day," Phillip confirmed.

"The two of us? You and me?" she said, her hopes tentatively rising.

What would they talk about? More important, what would she wear? Did he mean dinner in public? Or here? Frankie bit her lip, irritated at the surge of self-doubts. A hot, sexy, fantasy-inspiring guy was asking her out and all she could do was worry? What was wrong with her?

"I assume there might be a waiter, a chef, maybe other restaurant patrons," Phillip mused, his tone serious. But there was amusement in his eyes.

It was that humor, more than anything else, that relaxed her.

He was so cute, how could she say no?

"Friday would be lovely," she agreed, trying to sound gracious instead of giddy with delight.

"Seven?"

"Seven," she agreed, smiling. Then, realizing that there

were less than four days for shopping between now and then, she realized she'd better get it in gear. "I should go."

"Would you have thrown that?" he asked before she could leave, nodding toward her hand.

Frankie frowned at the plate, surprised the china hadn't melted from her body heat.

"Of course not," she said, a little horrified at the idea. Throw his own plate at him? How rude would that be? Besides, her grandmother would kill her.

So why did he look disappointed?

"You don't throw plates?"

"Not a Meissen, for crying out loud. And in the Banks house?" The image of her grandmother's reaction flashed through her mind, and Frankie shuddered. "Never."

His eyes glinted.

"Other plates? In another place?"

She wanted to say no. Tossing plates, throwing fits, it was so unladylike.

But she couldn't lie to him.

"Sometimes. But only if I'm really angry." Or frustrated. Or if her creativity was blocked. Or there were no cookies left in the cookie jar.

But there was no need to overshare.

She waited for him to rescind his dinner invitation.

Instead, he grinned.

The smile lit up his face, his green eyes glowing with something—Frankie didn't know what. But it made her want to strip off her clothes and climb on top of him. Or maybe that was just a residual effect from his kiss.

"I'll keep that in mind," he murmured.

She didn't understand him.

She knew he was right, that the choices they'd made before might not have been the best ones.

It had been easy to write that night in Vegas off to

creativity-inspired lust. A mission to break her artistic block. Even a chance to live out a long-lived fantasy.

But that had been one night. In Las Vegas. Thousands of miles away. Things didn't count the same there.

Here?

Here, they not only counted, they'd have a lasting impact on every part of her life. And she remembered the aftermath of their lovemaking. The intense need to hold him close and heal all of his hurts.

Here, their decisions could have a very scary effect on her heart.

Frankie opened her mouth to tell him dinner was a bad idea.

"Dressy or casual?" she heard herself asking instead.

God, what was wrong with her mouth? It had to be that kiss. Her lips were still under the influence.

"Does dressy mean sexy?" he wondered, his eyes skimming her body like a caress.

"It can if you want it to."

"Dressy, then."

Her head filled with dreamy visions of what she'd wear and how he'd react, Frankie could only nod. It took her two tries to get through the door and down the hall to the kitchen, but she finally made it.

"How'd Mr. Phillip enjoy dessert?" Nana asked, looking up from the vegetables she was chopping when Frankie set the plate in the sink.

"Good enough that he wanted more." Then, since she knew Nana didn't mean the same kind of second helping Frankie did, she crossed over to sneak a carrot curl and give her grandmother a smile. "He loved the pie. He said something about pumpkin, if you're up for making one."

"Definitely," Nana said with a smile.

"Do you need help with anything?" she asked her

grandmother. Better to get out of Nana's range when she was thinking such thoughts, in case she blurted one out.

"No, no. You go work. I'll be busy here for a while. I want to get started on the soup for tomorrow plus some other things."

Frankie hesitated. But it didn't take more than a glance into Nana's eyes to assure her that her grandmother was happy. She'd been in a good mood ever since she'd heard the Banks house would once again be occupied.

Maybe that was it, Frankie decided, brushing a quick kiss over her grandmother's cheek before heading out the door. Maybe Nana just needed to be busy, to feel needed. She made it through the door and halfway to the housekeeper's quarters without breaking into a dance.

Then she couldn't help herself.

She gave a hip-wriggling, fist-pumping, heels-in-the-air happy dance.

She had a date.

With Phillip Banks. *The* Phillip Banks, of her many and varied fantasies.

And this time, she hadn't even gotten him drunk first.

Frankie hugged her arms around herself, twirling in a circle.

Oh, it was going to be wonderful.

That last time had been all about sex. Which was all she'd wanted. The night had been amazing, the sex …well, *oh, my God*. A night to go down in history.

But Friday night?

A date might lead to sex, but it was about more than that. It was about romance.

Frankie stopped twirling so fast, she almost landed on her butt.

Romance?

Oh, wow.

Breathless and light-headed, she sat down on the lawn and buried her face in her hands.

This was it.

Frankie was sure divine intervention had sent Phillip here—in the guise of some highfalutin' muckety-muck in the Navy.

He was her fantasy guy.

He was her favorite distraction.

He was her inspiration.

And he was now available to inspire and distract her with fantasies for many weeks to come.

She shivered, her body getting tingles as she wondered how many positions they could try on how many surfaces in that length of time.

And, in between, how much jewelry she could make.

Was this it? The answer to her creative block?

Maybe the answer wasn't just adding another fantasy—albeit an incredible real-life one—to the playlist in her mind.

Maybe the answer was romance.

Tiny fingers of terror climbed her spine, whispering warnings of all of the emotional pitfalls and heartbreaking possibilities.

Frankie managed to ignore them, though.

All she had to do was focus on two simple things.

One, Phillip Banks had asked her on a date.

And two, if this worked, she would never have to make another Christmas ornament again.

7

"WHAT ABOUT THIS ONE?"

Frankie held up a simple black sheath, the soft fabric draping over the hanger. It screamed tasteful country club dinner, didn't it? She'd never been to the country club, but she imagined this was the kind of thing they wore there. Phillip hadn't said that was where they'd be going. But that was where he'd always taken dates when he'd lived here, so she figured it was a safe bet.

And so was this dress.

"Meh."

Meh?

Frankie held the dress out farther, squinting as she tried to imagine herself in it. It was a panty hose kind of dress, but she could buy those. It might be cute with some fuchsia stilettos or red patent pumps, but those would probably be out of place at such a classy restaurant.

"Maybe with the right jewelry?" she asked, tilting her head to the side. Something edgy, maybe geometric shapes chained at alternating lengths, draping to the waist?

Her heart danced at the idea, excitement curling in her belly. She could make that. She knew she could.

"Even the right jewelry won't fix that meh" came the bored response.

So frustrated her teeth ached from clenching them, Frankie glared at her friend. From the tip of her blue hair to the toes of her black Converse, Shayla dressed as if she had a religious objection to meh.

Which was why she'd brought her, Frankie reminded herself. It was a known fact that a woman's most vulnerable shopping times were after a breakup and before a first date. The only defense against ugly, tacky or slutty was an honest friend with a good eye.

Ugly, tacky, slutty *and,* apparently, meh.

Frankie looked at the dress again, then wrinkled her nose and put it back on the rack.

Shayla was right. It was totally meh.

Between the pushy saleswomen, the other shoppers and her lack of success finding a dress, Frankie had a serious headache. Of course, it might be from the cloying—and clashing—scent of each store. She walked out of each one with a new layer of fragrance clinging to her. A few more stores and she'd go home smelling like a whorehouse.

At least it would be an expensive, upscale one.

Frankie shuffled hangers on yet another clothes rack, trying to find something that said elegant chic. Something that would make Phillip drool, yet still be appropriate anywhere he took her, no matter how fancy.

"What am I going to wear?" Frankie groaned.

"Nothing in this place," Shayla told her, wrinkling her nose and waving away a saleswoman. "Unless you want to impersonate a complete bore."

Ignoring the saleswoman's offended huff, Shayla moved to a display of belts. Choosing one of supple black leather, she held it up to the light, then stepped in front of a mirror. Instead of wrapping the belt around her waist, though, she tied it like a choker around her neck.

"Why do you want to ditch your own style to dress like a cookie-cutter snob anyway?"

"I'm not ditching my own style." Much. "It's not like I'm changing my hair or getting a boob job, for crying out loud. I just want to find a suitable dress for the occasion."

"Thanksgiving is an occasion. My niece's bat mitzvah is an occasion. The half-yearly sale at Victoria's Secret is even an occasion." Shayla tilted her head to the side, then shifted the knot in the belt so the ends draped over her shoulder. "This is a date."

"Occasion. Date. Whatever. I need a dress." She'd gone through everything in her closet, and nothing was suitable for a formal Friday-night-at-seven-o'-clock date. Nothing.

Then she'd gone through Shayla's closet. She'd found a few things she loved, some that made her wince—who needed spikes on their bra?—and some that were an ode to ugly. But nothing she could wear Friday.

"You need to get past this," Shayla advised. "You are into the guy enough to date him, so date him as yourself."

"Get real." Frankie flipped through the size twelves hoping maybe something perfect in her size had been hung there by mistake. "If I've got the hots for the guy—and I seriously do—who else would I go as other than myself?"

"You always do this. You fixate on an image and try to fit into it like you're some kind of contortionist. Then when you get tired of being tied up in knots, you give up." Shayla pursed her lips, giving the leather belt one last look before unknotting it from her throat. "You usually throw a big fit when you give up, though. Which is what I stick around for. Nobody does tantrums like you, Frank."

Frankie rolled her eyes. One, maybe two justifiable outbursts in how many years and her own best friend labels her a tantrum thrower? What was she, in kindergarten?

She pulled a promising-looking dress from the rack. Pale blue satin with a fitted waist and three-quarter-length sleeves, it was pretty and the blue would suit her coloring.

"What about this? It reminds me of winter."

"Cold, icy and stiff?"

That might not be a bad thing. It brought to mind warming up, melting and, well, *stiff* spoke for itself. Frankie turned over the price tag and winced. Now, that was stiff.

"Let's get out of here," she decided, not sure if she was more irritated over not finding a dress or Shayla's assessment of her personality. She didn't change her personality to fit other people's expectations. She was who she was. So what if she changed her style from time to time to fit her interests?

And her current interest happened to be Phillip.

"There's nothing wrong with dressing appropriately for the occasion," she defended herself to Shayla as they buttoned themselves back into their coats to walk to the car. "If I took Phillip to a hoedown, I'd expect him to wear jeans, not a tuxedo."

"Have you ever gone to a hoedown?"

Frankie wrinkled her nose. She wasn't even sure what a hoedown was. But that wasn't the point.

"Okay, so if he attended an upscale art showing with me, I'd be justifiably embarrassed if he showed up in sweatpants."

"Sweatpants? Does Phillip Banks even own such a thing?"

He had to. The military was big on push-ups and other bodybuilding exercises, wasn't it? She'd seen his body. Yeah...he'd done some push-ups in his lifetime. Probably in sweatpants. Shirtless, though. So those muscles gleamed.

Whew. Her mouth was watering.

"What would he wear if you took him to a strip club?" Shayla pondered as Frankie unlocked her car.

"Is he going to be on stage?"

Shayla laughed, then grabbed the keys and, with a hip

bump, nudged Frankie aside. "I'll drive. You've got lust in your eyes."

That wasn't the only place she had lust. Frankie settled into her passenger seat and imagined Phillip stripping. Would he start from the top or the bottom?

"Listen to Shayla," her friend advised. "You're doing the exact same thing with this date that you did with your jewelry business."

And just like that, her lusty bubble burst.

"Failing?" Frankie asked, starting to pout.

"Trying to force yourself to fit some preconceived image of what you have to be to succeed. One day you're creating funky, out-of-the-box designs, the next you're following an uptight, boring business plan. That's what messed you up. That's why you're having so much trouble with designing," Shayla lectured. "Replace yawn-worthy dress for business plan, and here we are again."

"It's smart to go into business with a solid plan and set goals," Frankie defended herself, directly quoting the business counselor she'd seen when her custom jewelry had started taking off. "There's nothing wrong with wanting to succeed."

"Nope, nothing. Unless the pressure of trying to fit that ideal blows your creative juices all to hell." Shayla gave her a sideways glance. "I keep telling you, be yourself, do things your way. You'll be a lot happier."

"That's exactly what I'm doing. Believe me, there is no business plan, monthly quota or long-term contract involved in creating personalized silver and gemstone Christmas ornaments. The most pressure I have is counting correctly to make sure I have enough bells, trees and stars to get me through the week," Frankie said, tired of discussing her career. "So I should be ecstatic, right? After all, I'm about as low pressure as I can get and still pay the bills."

Shayla winced.

"Frankie—"

Time to change the subject.

"Where are we going?" she interrupted.

"Little shop I know. They're having a one-day sale."

The little shop turned out to be a funky retro consign-ment boutique.

"This is hardly the place to find an elegant dress for a fancy dinner date," she muttered as Shayla dragged her into the store.

But after three minutes inside, oh, how she wished it was. Edgy, chic and loud, the boutique was exactly the kind of place Frankie would normally shop at for herself.

But not for Phillip.

Since she couldn't say that without inciting another of Shayla's individuality lectures, Frankie made a show of looking through the clothes.

"Cute. Cute. Not cute. Darling. Perfect for summer," she muttered as she shuffled from one hanger to the next. The dresses were great, but too casual for her date.

"Found it," Shayla called, her voice raised to be heard over the pounding rock music.

Frankie turned to see what *it* was.

"Here," Shayla said, holding up a dress.

It was definitely a little black dress.

It had cap sleeves and a sweetheart neckline, a tucked waist and a pleated skirt that fell a few inches shy of the knees.

Frankie felt the buzz.

The sister of sexual awareness, the shopping buzz car-ried a lot of the same symptoms.

Frankie's heart raced. Her pulse skipped. She had to wrap her fingers into her palms to keep from reaching out to stroke the dress, certain she'd purr if she did.

"It's leather," she said, trying to talk herself out of her instant lust.

"So?" Shayla took it back, holding it in front of Frankie to see how it would look. "It's you."

Frankie wet her lips.

It was gorgeous. The pleats, the tucks, she knew it would showcase her curves in a sassy, but not slutty way. It would look awesome with her peep-toe booties.

Visions of the earrings she'd make to go with it filled her imagination. Soft swirls of silver with tiny garnet teardrops.

She knew she could make those earrings. Knew the insidious block wouldn't stand a chance against an image so vivid.

And they'd be perfect for the dress.

But...

It was leather.

She didn't think Phillip was a leather kind of guy.

Desperate for an excuse to say no, she looked at the price tag.

"Oh, my God." All those red lines through the prices. It had to be a sign from the shopping gods.

Shayla craned her neck around to look, too.

"Yeah, and my friend Margie is working. She'll give you her discount, so you can take another twenty percent off that."

The perfect dress and it wouldn't max her credit card?

Frankie reached out, her fingers millimeters from touching the leather.

Phillip had gone for her in a metal dress once.

Why not push his boundaries a little and see how he felt about leather?

PHILLIP WANTED HIS life back.

He wanted the barracks, he wanted mess hall, hell, he even wanted PT. He'd give anything for a hundred push-ups and a jog in the surf wearing full gear with a fifty-pound pack on his back.

He pulled up in front of the house on Friday evening and sighed. This wasn't his place. He was out of his element here, and he hated it.

Some men were born to teach.

They had a gift for imparting knowledge, a knack for engaging their students.

They understood learning styles, they connected with people, they made their subjects come to life.

Phillip wasn't one of them.

God, what a week.

He left the car in the driveway since he'd be going out again in an hour, and dammit, if he had to walk from the garage to the house he'd end up a snowman. The dash across the driveway alone had him shivering as he paused at the front door to shake the snowflakes off his overcoat.

Man, it was cold here. He'd been in California long enough to thin his blood. Either that or he was just getting old.

He pushed open the front door, letting it slam on the bitter cold and his equally bitter thoughts.

"Hello, Mrs. O'Brian," he said as the older woman stepped into the foyer. He set his briefcase on the floor to shrug off his coat.

"Welcome home, Mr. Phillip." She set a plate on the side table so she could take his coat before it dripped on the marble floor. "I know you said you'd be having dinner out tonight, so I brought you a snack."

A polite refusal at the ready, he glanced at the plate. And almost swallowed his tongue. Chocolate-chip pecan cookies? Homemade and fresh from the oven, if the scent was any indication. His hand was halfway to the plate when he remembered.

He had dinner plans in just over an hour.

Every day since he'd asked Frankie out to dinner, he'd told himself to cancel their date. But every time he considered it, he remembered that look in Frankie's expressive eyes. Pride and hurt mixed with just enough heat to keep him guessing which would win out if he tried.

So while the plan was unquestionably a bad idea, he was following through with it and they were having dinner. Which meant he didn't need a snack.

He'd had more to eat in the past few days than he usually ate in twice that amount of time. The mess hall had nothing on Mrs. O'Brian's cooking. As it was, he'd taken to doing PT in the morning, and again after lunch, to make sure he didn't outgrow his fatigues before he was back in California.

But the cookies smelled so good.

"I shouldn't," he muttered.

"You worked hard today, you deserve a little treat," Mrs. O'Brian said with a dismissive wave as she turned to leave. Then she tossed an impish smile over her shoulder that reminded him of her granddaughter. "Just don't ruin your appetite."

Wondering why he couldn't refuse the elder or younger Silvera women a damned thing, Phillip bit into his first cookie.

His taste buds went insane. He almost groaned at the combination of flavors that filled his mouth.

Delicious.

Still, he was a strong man. He could resist delicious.

Just like he would resist Frankie tonight.

After all, he was only going through with tonight's date because it would be rude and hurtful to cancel. Dinner, conversation and maybe a polite kiss good-night, that was all he'd be enjoying.

He eyed his cookie, promising himself it was the only temptation he'd be giving in to.

Grabbing the briefcase, he headed upstairs. His foot on the second step, he grimaced and turned around.

And grabbed the plate of cookies to take with him.

Yeah.

Those Silvera women were big on irresistible.

"Oh, wow," Frankie breathed as Phillip pulled up in front of the restaurant. The exterior was already decorated for the holidays. Two slender potted pines wrapped in red ribbon stood on either side of the entrance. Twinkle lights and poinsettias flanked the covered walkway.

"Is this okay?" he asked, frowning. The restaurant had come highly recommended by the three guys he'd asked. He'd made a point to ask married men, figuring anything they suggested would be wife-approved. He glanced at Frankie's face, trying to read her expression in the dim light.

Maybe those wives had lousy taste?

"This is so not the country club." Frankie's words trailed off as she craned her neck to look around him at the valet heading their way.

"Would you prefer the country club?" He couldn't imagine why. It was like eating in a fishbowl surrounded by piranhas. For all that this wasn't a real date—they wouldn't end the night with sex, he reminded himself—he'd still hoped for an enjoyable evening.

"The country club over one of the most romantic restaurants in the area? This place got a James Beard Award, did you know that? One of my friends dated a guy who worked here and she brought me their dessert menu. Oh, my God. The chocolate soufflé is supposed to be amazing."

His head spinning a little, Phillip shut off the engine. He wasn't sure when he'd picked up the ugly habit of second-guessing himself.

"Shall we start with dinner and work our way to the chocolate, then?" he suggested.

"Oh, yeah." Her smile was bright enough to light up the interior of the car, and warm enough to do weird things to Phillip's insides. His belly, he decided. And maybe a little south of that, he acknowledged. But not north. Definitely not north.

Baffled that he was actually thinking such crazy things, Phillip pushed open the door, handed his keys to the valet along with a tip, then rounded the car.

His frown still anchored to his face, he opened the passenger door.

"I wish you'd have let me pick you up at your place," Phillip said for the third time, holding out a hand to help Frankie from his car.

He'd never met anyone as hardheaded as her. Instead of letting him pick her up, or even giving him her address, she'd insisted on meeting him at the Banks house. Her stubbornness had pitted his resolve against manners that were so ingrained it hurt not to have her in for a predinner drink.

But that would be too intimate, he'd decided.

This was just a polite evening out. A way of assuring her that he wasn't a social snob. It wasn't really a date, and definitely wouldn't end in sex.

He was sure if he reminded himself of that last stipulation one or two or fifty times over dinner, everything would be fine.

Then, her slender fingers in his, Frankie swung her legs out of the car. Her satin coat slid open. And all his thoughts sputtered to a stop.

Oh, man.

His eyes locked on her feet. Were those supposed to be boots? They stopped just above her ankles to flare out like a collar, and her toes peeked out from the tips of the black leather. His gaze slowly climbed her legs. Such gorgeous legs. Long, subtly curved and deliciously bare. He wanted to press his lips against one, right there at the curve of her knee, and listen for her moan.

"My way was easier," she said, her words husky as she straightened, her body brushing lightly against his.

Phillip damn near moaned out loud.

He'd tried her way once and it might not be easier, but damn, it had been good. Need flashed through him, hot enough to melt the snow at his feet.

Then he frowned.

Wait.

What?

He had to clear his head of his lusty thoughts and re-play their conversation to figure out what she was responding to.

"'Doing the right thing might not be the easiest choice, but it's always the correct choice,'" he recited from rote.

Frankie arched an eyebrow, tilted her head and asked, "Is that a SEAL motto?"

"Banks motto," he muttered, feeling stupid repeating something he wasn't sure he even believed anymore. He'd bought into it at one time. Hell, he'd devoted most of his life to the idea. But what good had doing the right thing done him?

He escorted Frankie up the covered steps of the restau-rant and nodded his thanks to the doorman, who opened the heavy oak door. The restaurant didn't allow for walk-ins, so the cozy, plush lobby was empty. Phillip handed the coat-check girl his overcoat, but Frankie shook her head, her fingers tight on the closure of her satin one. His hand still cupping her elbow, more for an excuse to touch her than because he figured she needed to be steered toward their table, he gave his name to the maître d'.

They were led to a quiet corner, the candlelit table surrounded by potted plants and discreet screens. The banquette seating was cozy, but spacious, offering a chance for intimacy without demanding it.

"Your server is Michel and he'll be with you in just a moment," the man said quietly as they were seated. "Please enjoy your evening."

"This is gorgeous," Frankie observed, setting her small black purse on the seat next to her. Then her lips rounded in an O.

"What?" Phillip asked.

"I need to take off my coat." The black satin fabric caught the light as she slid from the booth to stand in front of him.

"So you told me a Banks motto. What are some SEAL mottos?" she asked, her eyes locked on his as she slowly released the buttons.

They were in a public place, a restaurant. Albeit a dimly lit and subtly-arranged-to-give-the-illusion-of-privacy restaurant. Still, it was public. And Frankie was only taking off her coat. Not stripping. But with each button she released, Phillip's heart beat a little faster. His breath tight in his chest, he couldn't tear his gaze from her fingers' journey down the front of her body.

Memories of those same fingers on his body added to the tension already lying heavy in his groin. They were not having sex, he reminded himself. Just because he bought her dinner didn't mean he was putting out.

"Phillip?" she prodded, giving a tiny shrug of her shoulders so the heavy coat fabric slid down to her elbows, then off into her waiting hand.

He could only stare.

She was incredible.

A vision in black leather.

Phillip tried to wet his lips, but his mouth was too dry. The supple material curved over her breasts, the neckline showcasing her cleavage and an intriguing necklace of twisted silver and red stones. Beneath her cleavage—and by God, there was a lot of it—the dress hugged her body to the waist before flaring out. The skirt was full enough to slide his hand under, to explore what she might possibly be wearing underneath. Frankie sat down, close enough to tempt him to satisfy his curiosity.

Phillip grabbed his glass instead.

"Mottos," he remembered, after swallowing the cold water. Imagining the ice working its way past his throat and down to his crotch, he finally cooled off enough to focus. "The SEALs have a few mottos."

"For instance?"

"'The only easy day was yesterday.'" Unlike how he felt about his father's oft-repeated belief, this one resonated.

"That doesn't sound comfortable," she observed, watching him intently.

"It isn't supposed to be. Comfortable is a half step away from careless. And careless gets people killed."

"I'm sure you're never careless."

His automatic *never* died on his lips, so Phillip took another drink of water. A year ago, he'd have unequivocally offered that "never." He couldn't say that anymore.

Now his history said otherwise.

Whether it had been his carelessness or someone else's machinations—and damn the Navy for giving him no information on which it was—didn't matter. All that mattered were the facts.

"Are there more mottos?" Frankie asked, her tone upbeat and her smile easy. But he could see the concern in her eyes.

Phillip didn't want pity—not even from himself.

So he shoved those self-indulgent thoughts aside and did what any intelligent man would do.

He leaned forward and focused all of his thoughts, all of his energy, on the gorgeous woman sitting next to him.

"One of my favorites is 'failure is not an option,'" he offered.

"Never?" She frowned, shaking her head so one red strand slid over her chest to lie in a tempting curl against her breast. "How is that possible? I mean, you can't control everything, right? Sometimes life—I mean, a mission—it just goes wrong. You're not a failure if it doesn't turn out the way you planned."

Refusing to travel down that road again, at least not over dinner, Phillip focused on Frankie instead. He could tell from the furrow of her brow and the disquiet in her eyes that she wasn't talking about *his* career. Before he could ask what she thought she'd failed at, their server arrived.

Phillip went through the motions, ordering wine and dinner, but as soon as Michel left, he returned to the subject.

"Failure isn't something not turning out a specific way," he said, wanting to reassure her. "Despite extensive planning, a stellar team of specially trained SEALs and state-of-the-art resources, a mission rarely goes as planned. That's why we always train for contingencies."

"Contingencies?" she echoed, looking as if she couldn't think of a single one for whatever she thought she'd failed at.

"Contingencies," he told her, unable to resist lifting her hand to his lips and brushing a reassuring kiss over her knuckles. "For instance, I haven't been able to get the taste of you out of my head. My objective for the evening was to taste you again. To do so, I'd planned to walk you to your front door after our dinner, where I'd kiss you good-night. A simple plan, perhaps, but one I was looking forward to."

Especially as it was all he'd planned to allow himself to enjoy.

Desire clear in her eyes, Frankie shifted her hand so that she could rub her thumb over his bottom lip.

"But I ruined your plan?" Her words were quiet, breathy. As if she needed to save up all of her oxygen for other things.

"The night isn't over yet," he assured her, drawing her thumb into his mouth before turning her hand to press a kiss to her palm. "And like I said, I'm trained in strategy. There's always more than one way to obtain any objective."

"So you have a backup plan?" she asked, the last word a whimper. Her pulse raced against his fingers. Her smile was a sultry invitation, her eyes filled with desire.

"I always have a backup plan."

"Do tell," she prompted, her free hand sliding over his thigh. His reaction was hard and fast.

Phillip had never talked dirty in public before.

He'd actually never talked dirty before.

But if her hand slid any higher, he'd seriously consider actually *doing* something dirty. Right there at the table.

Blood pounding, he leaned forward to take her mouth.

"Dinner, sir. Madam."

Damn it all to hell. Phillip released Frankie's hand, leaned back in his seat and closed his eyes. Several deep breaths later he was still pissed, but he was able to open his eyes and thank the waiter.

"This looks delicious," Frankie said.

She looked so chipper, he'd have thought her unaffected. Just as insult started to take hold, he saw her staring blankly at her salad, as if she didn't know what to do with it.

His lips twitched. He was glad to know he wasn't alone. Ready to try sublimating one hunger for another, Phillip made a show of picking up his salad fork. Frankie's lips pursed, then she smiled, lifted her fork and started eating.

"So you always have a backup plan?" Frankie said

PLEASE COMPLETE THE ENCLOSED
POSTCARD AND RETURN IT TODAY.

** ATTENTION READERS **

2 FREE BOOKS
ABSOLUTELY FREE • GUARANTEED

RECEIVE 2 FREE BOOKS
WHEN RETURNED

Plus
2 FREE
Mystery
Gifts!

To thank you for choosing to read one
of our fine books we'd like to send you
2 more excellent reads absolutely FREE!

2 FREE BOOKS

ABSOLUTELY FREE • GUARANTEED

2 FREE Books

We'd like to send you another 2 excellent reads from the series you're enjoying now **ABSOLUTELY FREE** to say thank you for choosing to read one of our fine books, and to give you a real taste of just how much fun the Harlequin™ reader service really is. There's no catch, and you're under no obligation to buy anything — EVER! Claim your 2 FREE Books today.

Plus you'll get 2 FREE Mystery Gifts (worth about $10)!

Pam Powers
for Harlequin Reader Service

VALUE:	COMBINED BOOK COVER PRICE:	POSTAGE DUE:
	Over $10 (US)/Over $10 (CAN)	$0

FRE

COMPLETE YOUR POSTCARD AND RETURN IT TODAY!

Plus 2 FREE Mystery Gifts!

2 FREE BOOKS

ABSOLUTELY FREE • GUARANTEED

▼ DETACH AND MAIL CARD TODAY! ▼

© 2014 HARLEQUIN ENTERPRISES LIMITED
® and ™ are trademarks owned and used by the trademark owner and/or its licensee. Printed in the U.S.A.

CLAIM YOUR FREE GIFTS

YES! Please send me my **2 FREE BOOKS** and **2 FREE GIFTS.** I understand that, as explained on the back of this card, I am under no obligation to purchase anything!

2
FREE
Books

M-8801-0792-MG

Affix sticker here

150/350 HDL GF6M

FIRST NAME

LAST NAME

ADDRESS

APT.#

CITY

STATE/PROV.

ZIP/POSTAL CODE

HB-N14-TF-13

If offer card is missing write to: Harlequin Reader Service, P.O. Box 1867, Buffalo NY 14240-1867 or visit www.ReaderService.com

BUSINESS REPLY MAIL

FIRST-CLASS MAIL   PERMIT NO. 717   BUFFALO, NY

POSTAGE WILL BE PAID BY ADDRESSEE

HARLEQUIN READER SERVICE

PO BOX 1867

BUFFALO NY 14240-9952

NO POSTAGE
NECESSARY
IF MAILED
IN THE
UNITED STATES

brightly as soon as the waiter left. "Is that another SEAL motto?"

"'Ready to lead, ready to follow, never quit,'" he said automatically, the words echoing faintly in his head through a fog of desire.

Frankie wet her lips, the glossy red glinting in the candlelight as she leaned forward.

"You know, I always think of you as a Banks. The scion of one of the oldest families in the area. Class president, valedictorian, prom king."

Phillip grimaced, pushing his salad plate away. Well, there went his appetite *and* all of his lusty thoughts, drowned in a wave of discomfiture.

"And you're still out with me?"

"Of course." She laughed. "There's nothing wrong with those things."

Sure, there wasn't. If a guy wanted to sound like an uptight snob with an overachiever complex.

Then again, if the shoe fits…

"But you're more than that," she said, as if reading his thoughts. She reached across the table and lightly traced her fingers over the back of his hand. "You're a SEAL."

"You knew that already," he reminded her.

"There's knowing, like in my head. Facts. Then there's knowing, like how it makes me feel in my body when I think about it."

Phillip wasn't the type to use his career to seduce women any more than he was the type to use his family name. But the look in Frankie's eyes was addictive. What he saw there was hot admiration, respect and a whole lot of lust.

He'd promised himself that this evening wasn't going to lead to anything. Yeah, he'd considered ending it in a kiss, but that was ingrained in his DNA. For most guys, a date equaled a kiss. But that was it for tonight. No sex.

He mentally repeated that vow.
No sex.
Then he looked at Frankie.
Yeah.
He emptied his glass of water.
That wasn't going to happen.

8

Oh, my.

Frankie had no idea how she got through the meal.

She'd never remember a single thing she ate, and she wasn't even sure if she'd had dessert or not.

She knew they must have driven home from the restaurant, but she didn't recall a thing about the trip.

Between the moment they'd first sat down—when Phillip had pressed his mouth to her palm, sending shivers of desire through her—and the moment he'd unlocked the front door of the Banks house, it was all a blur.

But now, standing on his front porch as he pushed the door open and gestured her inside, everything around her came to life. She wondered if she closed her eyes if she'd see the colors speeding past as time caught up with them.

"Is this your contingency plan?" she asked, setting her purse on the small marble table in the entryway before giving him a smile. Her hands went to the buttons of her evening coat, the satin fabric icy cold in contrast to the fire raging inside her.

Phillip's fingers covered hers, gently moving them aside and taking over the task of unbuttoning.

Frankie hoped her gulp wasn't audible.

He was so commanding.

So sexy.

And so overwhelming when he focused on her like he was. His green eyes were like lasers, watching her every move.

"This is one of my contingency plans," he acknowledged, his focus on her buttons now. With each one he released, his gaze became more intent. Frankie wouldn't be surprised if she climaxed right there in the foyer, just from that look alone.

"You have more than one contingency plan?" That he'd put that much thought into kissing her was so sexy. What else had he planned? And how long would it take him to get her coat off so she could find out?

"I think the time for planning is finished," he told her, his hands spreading her coat open. His gaze was as potent as a caress as it lingered on her breasts before sliding downward. He pushed the fabric off her shoulders, catching her coat before it hit the floor, and draped it over the chair next to her purse.

"It's time for action now," he said decisively.

Oh, baby.

Frankie knew firsthand how good he was at the action. And that had been when she'd done all the planning, leaving him in the role of spontaneously responding. She, on the other hand, had thought she was prepared for all the possibilities tonight might offer.

But she'd had no clue.

"What kind of action do you have in mind?" she asked, mentally wincing at the inanity of that question. All it'd needed was *big boy* tacked on the end to qualify as a cheesy pickup line.

Clearly she needed training in contingency planning.

"Would you like a drink?" he asked. He tucked his fingers under the bodice of her dress, just there where the neckline angled from her shoulders to her breasts.

"I'm not very thirsty," she whispered.

Frankie's breath caught and her stomach tightened. She didn't know her next move here. Before, she'd just gone with the fantasy. But this time?

This time—tonight? This wasn't a fantasy.

This was real.

She shivered.

Phillip hooked a finger in her dress, his knuckle sinking into her cleavage. His eyes locked on hers as he used his finger to pull her closer.

"Hungry?" he asked, his voice low.

"We just came from dinner," she reminded him, her eyes on his mouth. His lips were so close.

"So we did," he murmured before brushing those lips over hers.

Soft. So soft.

His tongue slid along the seam of her mouth, teasing one corner and then the other.

Delicious. So delicious.

His hands were warm on her back, his body hard against hers.

He leaned back, just enough to look into her eyes. He must have liked what he saw there, because he gave an infinitesimal nod.

"Upstairs."

His quiet words weren't a question. She wasn't even sure they were a suggestion. To her body, they were a command.

One she couldn't refuse.

"Take me," she suggested, her smile naughty as she tilted her head toward the staircase.

"As soon as we get upstairs," he promised. For now, he took her hand. Frankie focused on his butt as he led the way up the stairs. The man had such a nice ass.

At the top of the stairs, he angled right, then left again.

How big was this place? Then he stopped. His hand on the knob, he gave her a questioning look.

As if she'd turn and run now.

Even if she wanted to, Frankie didn't think she could find her way out.

Which meant she was here to stay.

At least for tonight.

She tilted her head toward the door in answer.

Phillip swung it open with a push of his hand.

"I've never seen your bedroom," she said.

He didn't give her a chance to see it now either.

Three steps inside, he had her back against the wall, his body pressed against her as his fingers tunneled into her hair. His hands cupping the back of her head, Phillip angled her face for his kiss.

His mouth was wild.

His tongue raced, as if he were in a contest to see how fast he could turn her on. Two seconds was all it took, Frankie decided.

He was voracious.

And so was she.

Needing to feel his warm, hard flesh, Frankie pulled at his shirt. She heard a ping. Button? She didn't care, except that it gave her the access she'd been searching for.

She groaned against his mouth when her fingers found his chest. She scraped her fingers through the light dusting of hair, following the trail down to his belt.

"So good," she panted against his mouth. "You make me feel so good."

"I promise I'm going to make you feel so much better."

"I like a man who has the confidence to make a promise like that." She laughed, her head falling back against the wall while he scattered kisses across her jawline.

"I never fail," he assured her, his hands wrapping

around her waist before sliding up the tight leather to cup her breasts. "Especially not a woman as incredible as you."

Oh.

Frankie melted. She couldn't help it. She was pretty sure that was the sweetest thing a guy had ever said to her.

"I almost swallowed my tongue when you dropped your coat, standing there in this sexy leather getup," he said, pushing her hair aside and kissing the sensitive flesh beneath her ear.

Heat coiled low in her belly.

He nipped at her earlobe, sending that heat surging through her body with the intensity of a small orgasm.

Frankie whimpered, then desperately grabbed on to control.

When she went over, she wanted him with her.

She needed to know she'd driven him as wild as he drove her.

Which meant a little teasing was in order.

"You like? And I was worried about wearing this dress," she murmured as his lips meandered down her throat and over her shoulder.

"Afraid my blood pressure couldn't take it?" he asked, his words vibrating against her skin, sending echoes of delight through her body.

Frankie slid her hand down his chest, over the delicious planes of his flat abs, then along his zipper. With a soft moan of approval, she cupped the hard length of his erection as it strained the fabric.

"I'd say your blood pressure is doing just fine." She laughed breathlessly.

She felt the cool air, then the smooth wall against her bare back before she realized he'd found her zipper, too. Using his lips, he pulled one cap sleeve down to bare her shoulder.

"A testament to this dress," he told her, pushing the

other sleeve off, too. The weight of the leather sent the dress plummeting to her feet. "Oh, yeah, I love this dress."

"I'm so glad." Her laugh ended on a moan when Phillip's hand cupped her breast, his fingers hot through the red lace of her bra. "I worried that you'd think it was too out there. It's definitely not a country-club dress."

"I've been out with women who wear country-club dresses. I like yours much better. I like you much better."

His words broke through the sensual haze surrounding her, making Frankie smile. She combed her fingers through his short, silky hair, knees trembling when he knelt in front of her.

"Why?" she asked. But before the word left her lips, she'd totally forgotten what she was asking.

God, he felt so good. She stroked her palms over his shoulders, reveling in the muscles there. The man was incredible. She could spend hours, days even, exploring his body.

"You're out of the ordinary. Different." His lips left a hot, damp trail down her belly, his fingers hooking the elastic of her panties on either side and sliding them down her legs.

"You're like nobody I've ever known," he said, his breath warm on her thigh. "The perfect escape."

Was that a good thing? Bells rang out a warning somewhere in the back of Frankie's head. But then Phillip's mouth reached its destination, his shoulders pressing her legs apart a little more, and she forgot everything.

Everything but how he made her feel.

GOD, SHE FELT GOOD.

Phillip looked up the length of Frankie's lush body, blown away at the intensity of his reaction to her.

Wanting hers to be just as strong, he grazed his lips up her thigh, inching closer and closer to heaven with each kiss. Her fingers kneaded his shoulder. He could feel the tension in her body, the shaking of her knees.

His eyes locked on her face, he slid his tongue over her swollen folds. Circling, teasing, then sucking.

She gasped. Her face was tight, her legs trembling.

He pressed his hand against her butt for support. Then, unable to resist any longer, Phillip slipped his tongue inside, his free hand slipping between them to tease her bud.

She tasted so good.

His tongue swirled, plunged, savored.

Need pounded through him. Still holding her upright with one hand, he swept the other up her body to cup her breast, his fingers teasing her nipple through the lace.

She flew over.

"Ooh." Her pleasured gasp rang out, her fingers gripping his hair as her body convulsed. His tongue slowed, prolonging her satisfaction. She shuddered twice more, each cry of delight sliding over his body like a caress.

He felt her knees give way.

Before she sank an inch, he was on his feet, sweeping her into his arms.

"Wow," she breathed, her head falling against his shoulder, one arm around the back of his neck while the other pushed his shirt out of the way to tease its way over his chest.

He shoved the covers aside before laying her across his bed. Frankie angled herself onto one elbow. A luscious vision in nothing but a red lace bra, she gave him a languorous look.

His eyes locked on hers and he tore his clothes off, pausing only to grab a condom from the bedside table before joining her.

She lay back, her red hair spread over his pillowcase, her hands racing over his body, nails scraping down his chest, over his stomach. Then she grasped his erection with her fingers.

Phillip saw stars.

Control. He wasn't going to lose control.

He reached between her breasts, unhooking the fabric of her bra, forcing her to release him so he could slide it off.

"Gorgeous," he murmured, skimming his fingers over her silken shoulder and across the swell of her breast before rubbing her pebbled nipple.

She gasped.

The sound flipped his switch.

And blew his control all to hell.

Phillip's hands roamed over her body. Cupping, grasping. He took her mouth in huge, ravenous bites. Her fingers dug into his chest. She wrapped one leg around his, her boot sliding over his thigh, the heel digging into his butt.

That she was still wearing her boots sent him over the edge.

Crazed with need, he barely remembered the condom before angling himself over her.

Frankie's breath was labored, her hair wild and her eyes glazed. Poised over her body, arms rigid, Phillip reveled in the sight of her, watching her face as he sought entry in her welcoming heat.

He wasn't a religious man, but he was sure this was what heaven felt like.

He sank into Frankie's warmth, watching the delight and excitement dance over her face. She was so expressive. So alive.

His body clenched.

So wet. So tight. So damned good.

Her fingers clutched at him, heels digging into the small of his back as Frankie met each thrust with a whimper.

Phillip leaned down, sucking one cherry nipple into his mouth.

Frankie bucked, arching her back as she cried out.

The feel of her contractions, the sound of her pleasure, the sight of her gratification were too much.

Phillip plunged deeper.

Once.

Twice.

Then he exploded.

His breath labored, the power of his orgasm still echoing through his body, he shifted his weight off Frankie. He took a second to deal with the condom and her boots. He pulled the blankets over them, then wrapped his arms around her.

Still trembling, she pressed her body against his, her leg wrapping around his thigh and her fingers tight against his back.

Even as her breath evened out and her body grew heavy with sleep, she still clung to him.

Phillip had never had anyone want him so much.

She'd climaxed three times. He'd counted.

Yet she still acted as if she couldn't get enough of him.

Depleted and a little emotionally overwhelmed, he willed himself to follow Frankie to sleep.

As he drifted off, he admitted to himself that for most of his life, his value had been as a Banks, then later as a SEAL. Those were his only identities.

With Frankie, he was just a man.

It was enough to blow his mind.

Burying his face in her hair, he breathed her in.

Just before sleep engulfed him, he realized that if he wasn't careful he might actually start believing in that fairy tale called love.

FRANKIE WOKE SLOWLY, reluctantly, not wanting her delicious erotic dream to end. As long as her eyes were closed, she could convince herself that she hadn't dreamed the night. She didn't doubt the three orgasms her body assured her it had enjoyed. But she'd awoken many a time after dreams so hot, so intense, she was sure they were the real thing.

And every single time she'd found herself alone in bed.

She did appreciate her vivid imagination providing her with such delightful nighttime entertainment. But she was pretty sure she'd cry if she opened her eyes and discovered that her date with Phillip had been but a dream.

Appreciating the vast merits of avoidance, Frankie threw one arm over her eyes to block out any future sunlight, then snuggled deeper into the pillow, ready to drift off again.

Then she felt it.

Excitement stirred in her belly. She barely dared to breathe as she slowly slid her hand down along the side of her body to see what was brushing against her hip.

Was it...?

Her fingertip slid across hard velvet.

Yep.

That was a penis.

Her arm still thrown over her eyes, she slowly turned her head to peek. And saw a chest. A hard, sculpted, gorgeous chest.

Oh, yeah.

It was Phillip's penis.

She spread her fingers and looked up.

Awake, Phillip Banks was gorgeous but a little intimidating.

Asleep, he looked like an angel—albeit, a warrior angel. One of those winged guardians, ever vigilant and ready to do battle even in his sleep.

Suddenly, his face tightened. As if her thoughts had trigged a battle only he could see, he drew back his lips in a ferocious grimace. She felt rather than heard his moan. As if whatever it was hurt too much for him to give it voice.

Frankie's breath knotted in her chest. Wanting to comfort him but terrified of setting loose whatever he was fighting, she reached up to lightly graze the backs of her fingers over his chest.

His face relaxed instantly. The scowl faded and his breathing evened out.

Frankie frowned.

Had she imagined the pain?

As stealthily as she'd first reached out, she slid her hand back. Her heart still pounding, she turned her head away from Phillip.

What had he gone through that would torture him like that?

Until now, there had been no sign of the aching misery she'd seen in his eyes that night in Las Vegas. She'd actually convinced herself she'd imagined it. That she'd dreamed it up as an excuse to believe he might need her.

Now she didn't know what to think.

Except to know that he'd reject any attempt she made to talk about it or offer comfort.

Let it go, she told herself. *Focus on what we have between us. Hot sex. Wildly hot, extremely satisfying sex.*

Determined to get her thoughts back on track, she shifted onto her side, careful not to disturb Phillip.

The snow had turned to rain. Frankie watched the drops throw themselves against the glass of the French doors, then slowly slide down. Sort of like her and Phillip, she thought with a deep sigh. She wasn't sure which of them had thrown themselves at whom first, at least, not this time. Her fingers curved over the back of his hand where it wrapped over her waist.

But she'd felt like one of those raindrops, going splat all over the place.

Frankie's lips twitched.

Wasn't she the poet?

After their lovemaking in Las Vegas, she'd seen swirls and shapes of all kinds, so many inspiring images that every time she'd closed her eyes she'd been overwhelmed by the creative possibilities. She hadn't been able to wait to get back to her studio.

This time? She was equating the most incredible sex of her life to the splat of a raindrop.

Maybe because her body was reliving the memory of the incredible things he'd made her feel. Her imagination was wallowing in the image of the two of them wrapped around each other in Phillip's bed.

Right now.

Tomorrow.

Next year.

Whoa.

Love?

Now, that was crazy thinking.

Almost as crazy as imagining Phillip might need her.

Frankie scowled at the rain. The stupid weather was putting silly thoughts in her head. The two of them a real couple? That would never happen. She didn't even want it to happen.

Fantasies and mind-blowing sex aside, they had nothing in common. There was no way a relationship could work between a flaky, failing jewelry designer and a rich-boy, dedicated SEAL.

Her eyes swept the room. Other than the clothes they'd stripped off each other, there wasn't a thing out of place. No clutter in the tan room. A bland tan, she realized, frowning at the walls.

Clearly they were totally wrong for each other. She was creatively messy and needed to be surrounded by color. He was obsessively tidy, and unless he decorated the inside of his footlocker like a rainbow, she'd bet camouflage was as close to color as he got.

They probably didn't even like the same books or movies or music. She sucked in her bottom lip, trying to remember if they'd discussed any of those things on their date.

The whole evening had been shrouded in a sensual fog.

That only proved that they were all about the sex. Sure, the chemistry they shared was hot—incendiary even. But anything that hot couldn't last long.

Determined to prove that to herself—and try to douse those flames before she started to read too much into what they meant—Frankie quietly turned over.

She brushed her fingers softly over his cheek.

And smiled when he murmured her name.

Then she proceeded to kiss her way down his body so she could wake him in a way that would turn those flames into a bonfire.

9

IT MIGHT HAVE been hours, it might have been days later when Frankie woke again. She stretched, delight filling her body. She didn't have to look to know that Phillip wasn't there this time.

But she did anyway.

She ran her hand over the indention on his pillow, then, after a quick glance to make sure she was alone, hugged it to her. Emotions washed over her in gentle waves, sweetly poignant.

Then she realized what those emotions were.

Frankie's eyes popped open and she threw the pillow so hard it bounced off the wall.

Groaning, she shoved herself into a sitting position, resting her head on her knees.

What had she done?

Her morning had been so hot it sizzled, but it hadn't done its job. Because here she was, all giddy and filled with joy, falling for Phillip.

She pressed her knees harder against her closed eyes, hoping the pressure would erase the crazy thought from her head.

Instead, she saw rays of color. Twisting color, coiling

around a fat gemstone. She concentrated, trying to bring the image into focus.

"Oh," she breathed in wonder. Onyx, roughly cut and tumbled. The metal burnished to reflect light like a prism, sending off rainbows. The vision coalesced in her mind, spinning and turning so she could see it from all sides.

It wasn't just the end result she was seeing, but the step-by-step execution. As sure as she knew her own name, Frankie knew she could make the piece actually work.

Unlike every other time inspiration had hit in the past year, she wasn't afraid that this burst of creative energy would disappear in a poof of disappointment.

This time it felt solid. It felt real.

But the crazy thought was still there.

Despite knowing they had no future, she was terrifyingly close to falling for Phillip. A part of her wanted to run. She was out of the bed and searching for her underwear before it hit her.

Running wasn't going to make any difference.

No matter how far she got from him, Phillip would still star in her dreams.

Fine, then.

If she couldn't escape it, and there was no point in denying it, she would simply do what she did best.

Enjoy it.

Since Phillip was nowhere to be seen—thank God—she used his bathroom and stole a crisp white shirt from his closet.

Buttoning it as she went, Frankie made her way down the stairs, the rich scent of coffee luring her onward. Telling herself the nerves dancing in her stomach were just preparation for enjoyment, she took a deep breath, ran her fingers through her hair, then stepped into the kitchen.

And almost melted into a puddle right then and there.

Thankfully, Phillip was focused on the newspaper on

the counter in front of him and his back was to her, giving her a second to gather her composure.

And to enjoy the view. Her gaze traveled from the breadth of his shoulders down the length of his back to the sweetness of his butt. He looked as casual as she'd ever seen him in jeans and a thermal shirt; both hugged his muscles and made the most of his gorgeous body.

She wanted to eat him up with toast.

"Morning," she greeted him instead, wishing she'd taken the time to find her purse and put on a little makeup.

He turned around. His polite smile shifted into something warmer. He looked her over with such intensity that Frankie's toes curled against the hardwood floor.

"Good morning," he finally said. Barely taking his eyes off her, he poured coffee into a cup, then lifted it in question. "How do you like it?"

Any way he wanted to give it to her.

"Just black, thanks," she said instead.

Her eyes locked on his. Desperate to kiss him but just as eager to keep things steady, she took the cup, then sipped.

Heaven.

He did good coffee.

"Aren't you worried your grandmother will object to you wandering around wearing only my shirt and your underwear?" Phillip asked, grinning to assure her that he didn't mind in the least.

"Nah." Frankie took a long swallow, letting the caffeine work its magic. "She decided to spend the weekend with my aunt."

"Your grandmother is gone all weekend?" he repeated, his gaze focusing on her cleavage, displayed in all its glory by his barely buttoned shirt.

"My grandmother is gone until Monday night," she said, smiling over her coffee cup as her finger played with a button.

"Is that a fact?" he asked, looking as if he wanted to deal with the button himself.

"It is. I have three days to do anything and everything I want," she told him in a teasing tone. "Anytime and anywhere, even."

"Yeah?" His eyes slumberous with desire, Phillip brushed his finger along the edge of the shirt, tracing it from the collar to that button just between her breasts.

"Yeah." Before she could suggest a few things he might want to try, though, her stomach gave a loud grumble.

Frankie winced, and then relaxed when Phillip's stunned expression turned to laughter.

"There's something labeled *breakfast* in the refrigerator. Actually there are a few things labeled *breakfast,* more labeled *lunch* and enough dinner to feed a platoon." Phillip handed her a list off the counter. "Her concern that I'd starve aside, I don't remember Mrs. O'Brian mentioning that she'd be gone."

"It probably slipped her mind," Frankie said, looking at the list.

"Holy cow, we're in luck!" she exclaimed, tossing the paper onto the counter and diving for the fridge.

She didn't need to see the neatly typed label stuck to the top of the lid to know which casserole dish to pull out.

Practically dancing with excitement, she opened the lid.

"Oh, man, this is the best casserole in the world. Bread, eggs, sausage, cheese and all kinds of other stuff she won't tell me." Frankie cut out two portions and slid them onto microwave-safe plates. She knew it should be warmed in the oven, but she was too hungry to wait. "She hardly ever makes it."

"Why don't you just make it yourself, then?"

"I can't," she admitted, watching the plate spin in the microwave. She hated that there were things she loved that she simply couldn't have whenever she wanted.

"Your grandmother won't share her recipes?"

"Not her favorite ones." Frankie wrinkled her nose, then added, "At least, not with me. She's given this one to my cousin and my aunt, though."

Refilling his coffee, Phillip lifted the carafe, silently asking her if she wanted any. The microwave beeped, and Frankie exchanged one plate for the other, nodding yes to the coffee.

"Since it's obviously a favorite of yours, why won't she tell you how to make it?"

"Because I suck as a cook. Nana considers it sacrilegious for one of her recipes to be attached in any way to my cooking."

He frowned. "You can't cook?"

"Can you?"

He opened his mouth, then caught a good look at her expression and wisely clamped his lips together.

"I make up for my lousy cooking skills with excellent baking ones, though," she defended.

"Isn't that the same thing?"

"Not quite." Frankie took the second dish from the microwave and carried both to the small corner table. She noticed the hesitant look on Phillip's face, but before she could ask, he grabbed the utensils and the coffee. She waited until they were both seated, then continued.

"Cooking is this," she said, pointing at the golden casserole with her fork. "Breakfast, lunch, dinner. Those require cooking."

"And baking?"

"The most important meal of the day. Dessert." Frankie wiggled her brows, rubbing his leg with one bare foot. "And believe me, I rock dessert. Especially cookies."

"Cookies," he said, his tone so doubtful she wondered if he'd ever eaten one.

"Cookies. I am the cookie queen."

"Yeah? You're going to have to prove it, cookie queen."

"You're on."

"We'll see if your cookies are any match for this… whatever this is that has you so excited." He gave his plate a doubtful look, pushing the bread around with his fork.

"Try it. If you don't like it, I'll be happy to finish it for you."

"You'd eat that huge casserole all by yourself?"

"I usually have to wait for Christmas morning for this. And even then, I have to share. Nana's big on sharing." Frankie gave a delicate shudder before scooping up her first bite. Steam curled from the fork, so she gave it a cursory blow before shoving it in her mouth.

Mmm.

From the look on Phillip's face, he agreed with her.

Not another word was said until their plates were all but licked clean. Phillip leaned back in his chair, looking a little shocked at how much he'd eaten.

"Your cookies are going to have to be pretty good to beat that," he decided.

"As soon as you taste my cookies, you'll be begging for more," she said as she propped her elbows on the table and leaned forward. The move left her shirt gaping open, a fact that Phillip clearly appreciated.

"I hate to burst your bubble, but I've never begged for anything in my life." As soon as the words were out, his eyes changed. Filled with a pain so intense Frankie had to bite her lip to keep from crying.

"Shall we bet?" she asked in a cheery tone, desperate to chase those shadows away.

"Bet?" Bafflement replaced pain on his face, and he shook his head. "How would we do that?"

"You poor, sheltered man. Don't tell me you've never bet before either."

"Some might say I place a bet every time I put on my uniform," he pointed out.

The enormity of the stakes he played for hit Frankie

like a sledgehammer. How did he and other men like him do that? Especially when it was obvious that sometimes they lost the bet.

How did their loved ones handle it?

She was only just infatuated with him—something she'd do well to keep reminding herself of—and the thought of what he must face, the choices he had to make, filled her with terror.

Needing a second, she busied herself with clearing the table and carrying their plates to the sink.

Light.

She needed to keep things light.

For herself, but more so for Phillip.

He hadn't had enough light in his life.

Cookies. She swallowed back the tears, turned off the water and dried her hands.

"I'll make cookies this afternoon," she said as she turned to face him with a bright smile. Christmas cookies. Nothing was as cheerful as Christmas cookies.

"Cookies? Is that what we're somehow going to bet on?"

He was so cute and confused.

Frankie couldn't help it—she just had to kiss him. Then, when he kissed her back, she curled into his lap.

"I'll bet you that after tasting my cookies, you love them so much you're willing to do whatever I want for the rest of the night," she challenged.

"I'm willing to do whatever you want right now." Proving his claim, he slid his hand up her bare thigh, then back down again.

Desire unfurled low in her belly before seeping through her body. His body's response against the back of her leg assured her that he felt the heat, too.

Then she glanced at the clock and groaned.

"Oh, man, I almost forgot. The Pettrys will be here any time. I promised Nana I'd meet them."

"Who and why?" he asked, pulling his gaze from her cleavage but not removing his hand from her thigh. A hand that was getting closer and closer to convincing her to ignore her promise.

"Mr. Pettry used to be the gardener until he retired. The other Pettrys are his sons." When Phillip tapped her thigh, she remembered the rest of his question. "They're bringing the Christmas decorations from storage."

His hand stilled.

"Why?"

"Because we need to start thinking about decorating." Figuring the sight of her in a barely buttoned shirt might be a little rough on the old man's heart, Frankie reluctantly left Phillip's arms. "I'll get dressed, then we can get started."

"Started doing what?" On his feet as well, Phillip suddenly looked every inch a Banks. Distant. Cool. Regal.

Frankie frowned at him.

"Just what I said. Decorating. Why? Is that a problem?" She crossed her arms over her chest, not sure why she suddenly felt so defensive.

"Yes."

"Why?"

"It's a waste of time. I don't understand the need to haul out a ton of dust catchers, spend hours draping them around the house, only to haul them back down again in a month." Phillip's frown matched her own.

"Because it's Christmas." ·

"So?"

Frankie opened her mouth to list all the reasons why decorations mattered, how special the season was and why he should quit acting like a brat.

Then, standing in the spacious Banks kitchen with its state-of-the-art appliances, the view of a sparkling pool and an acre of green grass out the window, it hit her.

Phillip had never celebrated Christmas.

Oh, she was sure the Banks family had gone through the motions. The house had always been decorated, an elegant dinner for thirty served and expensive gifts exchanged.

But that wasn't celebrating.

Poor guy.

She'd show him what celebrating was.

She'd show him Christmas.

Her heart filled with too many emotions to identify, Frankie stepped forward to tell him how great the next several weeks were going to be. But Phillip held up one hand before she could say a word.

"You'll have to handle it yourself, I'm afraid." Phillip made a show of looking at his watch. "I've got to report to the training center."

Sure he did.

Frankie watched him leave.

"Don't think you're getting out of this," she muttered, turning on her heel and stomping in the opposite direction to find her clothes. "I'm introducing you to Christmas one way or the other. And you'll damn well like it."

GOD, HE HATED THIS.

What in the hell had happened to his tidy, controlled, well-planned life?

Frustration powering every step, Phillip paced from one end of his makeshift office to the other.

Here he was, stuck in Maryland instead of implementing the biggest mission of his career. And it was all because the powers that be—powers whose judgment he'd once respected—had deemed him unqualified to participate.

Stuck in a house that stood as a reminder of family expectations and demands. Demands that weighed on him, heavier every day. Expectations that he had clearly not reached.

Stuck at the training center on his day off.

His stride hitched a little at that one.

Yeah, that one was on him.

He dropped into the chair in front of his desk, scrubbing his hands over his face.

Everything had been great. Until Frankie had started talking about Christmas. First it was decorating, next it would be entertaining. Finding the perfect gift.

God, he hated the holidays.

Now more than ever for their role in disrupting a morning that had started off with great sex.

Phillip gave up on doing his paperwork and headed for the gym. An hour later, still frustrated and sporting a bruise on his chin because he'd let his guard down while sparring, he got in the shower.

He considered hitting the shooting range, but in his current state of mind he'd only be a menace. Instead, Phillip headed back to his office. He returned a few salutes along the way, but nobody spoke to him.

Not surprising. He was a superior officer with a reputation for being a stickler for protocol. His call sign wasn't "sir" for nothing.

But for the first time in his life, he felt lonely.

He missed his team.

Feeling like a sap, tired of being bombarded by all these unwelcome emotions, Phillip stood in the middle of his office with his fists clenched. He wanted to pound the desk, to throw it out the window. His desolation was drowned by fury, now as familiar as his once-touted control.

It took three harsh breaths and a reminder that he was a SEAL for him to regain control. Another breath to shake off the nasty buzzing left by the onslaught.

Damned if practice didn't pay off. It usually took him a lot longer to shake off these feelings. He mentally dismissed the incident, then looked around the cramped beige room.

What to do next… He debated whether he should work

on his lousy presentation or head home and deal with the godforsaken Christmas decorations.

The phone rang.

"Banks," he said as he picked it up, wondering who could be calling.

"Would that be *the* Phillip Banks, super SEAL?" a husky female voice asked.

It was as if the sun peeked out from behind the storm clouds. It didn't chase them away, but it did offer a welcome warmth.

"Lara?" Phillip found himself grinning as he dropped into the chair. "What are you calling for?"

"Can't a sister call her big brother without a reason?"

Phillip pondered the question, then shook his head.

"Pretty sure this is the first time you've ever called, so I'd have to say no."

"Not true. I called you for a ride home when I was fourteen and that creep dumped me for not putting out."

"But that was a reason."

"Aren't you smart." She laughed. "Fine, so I have a reason."

Phillip waited. He could almost hear her teeth grinding as Lara did the same thing. He knew she could out-stubborn him. Hell, Lara could out-stubborn the whole world. But he had a wealth of patience at his fingertips.

"What's the reason?" he asked.

"The holidays, of course."

"What?" Phillip groaned, pressing his fingertips against his eyelids. "Why? What is with everyone wanting to talk about the holidays all of a sudden?"

"Because it's holiday time," she said. "Just because we don't like them doesn't mean the rest of the world isn't on board."

"I'm pretty sure if the rest of the world jumped off a

bridge, we'd wave goodbye instead of joining them," he pointed out.

"Oh, now, that's cold," Lara said with a delighted laugh. "And usually I'd agree."

"But you're making an exception now," he mused, relaxing as he kicked his feet out in front of him and leaned back in the chair. "The more important question would be *why* you want to talk about this with me?"

"I married Dominic Castillo."

"Indeed you did, in what can only be described as the weirdest wedding ever." He sat upright, tension gathering in his shoulders. "Is there a problem? Has he done something?"

"No, of course not," she dismissed easily. Easily enough to allay Phillip's concern. He settled back in the chair again, not quite ready to relax.

"Then what's the issue? Is this about my not staying for cake?" His reason for leaving had been much more delicious than cake, he remembered.

"No, but I wouldn't mind hearing the reason you skipped out. Rumor is you left with a woman," she teased, sounding half amused, half intrigued.

Phillip tensed again. Not because he was ashamed of his relationship with Frankie. He simply didn't like the idea of her being the subject of gossip.

"Well?" Lara prodded.

"Well, what? Don't you have rumors to go on?"

"SEALs are lousy at gossip. I heard there was a woman involved from one of Castillo's cousins, but apparently nobody else saw or heard a thing. To hear the team tell, you might not have even been in Las Vegas." Her huff came through loud and clear.

Phillip grinned. Damned if the team didn't come through time and time again.

"Okay, fine, don't tell me anything. I'll find out eventually. Anyway, that's not the reason I called." He heard her take a deep breath. "I have to spend Christmas with Dominic's family. His entire family. Do you know how many of them there are? Dozens. Probably hundreds. They're all friendly and talkative and, you know, touchy-feely. They're always giving hugs or patting each other on the back. They actually like people."

Frankie was the same way. Except he wasn't uncomfortable when she touched him. He enjoyed her bubbly conversation and easy way with people.

But understanding didn't mean he should let Lara off the hook.

"Scared?" he teased, enjoying his feisty sister's discomfort in a way only a brother could.

"I'm not scared," she snapped. "I'm simply nervous."

"If I were stuck in a room filled with people who talk as much as Castillo, I'd be nervous, too." Phillip laughed.

"Will you come?" she blurted out. "Please, join us."

Hell, no.

"I'm not flying to California to spend Christmas with strangers."

"I'm not a stranger."

He could hear it in her voice. The plea for reassurance that she was right.

"No," he agreed softly. "You're my sister. But you're building a new life with your husband. This is for the two of you to do."

"The two of us and dozens of others," she muttered.

"Lara, you've dined with senators, danced for aristocrats. You've kicked bullies' asses and stood up to the biggest hard-ass around, our father. You can do this."

"That was before," Lara said, her voice as close to a whine as he'd ever heard. "This matters. I don't want to disappoint Dominic."

"I don't think that's possible. The guy loves you, Lara.

You could declare a war on Christmas and outlaw beer and he'd still love you."

"That's a lot of love," she said with a husky laugh.

The janitor walked in, stopped short at the sight of Phillip, then turned to leave. Phillip lifted one finger to halt his departure.

"I've gotta go," he told Lara, actually regretting putting an end to their conversation.

"Hey," she said quietly before he could hang up.

"What?"

"Take care, okay?"

Phillip stared at the phone, the old-fashioned dial tone echoing through the room.

Take care.

If she'd reached through the line to grab him up into a big hug and declared the depth of her sisterly love for him, he couldn't have been more surprised.

Or more touched.

He blew out a breath and carefully returned the receiver to its cradle.

It was weird, he decided, gathering his paperwork to leave.

They'd grown up practically strangers in the same house, Lara totally focused on dance, him on school. He'd been at Annapolis when she'd run away at sixteen, but it had been a year before he'd actually found out. Even then he only had because Mrs. O'Brian had told him when he'd gone home for the holidays.

Now he felt a love for his sister he hadn't known was there. Seeing her happiness, her devotion to her husband, it gave him hope that he had that inside him, as well.

He thought of Frankie back at the house, wearing nothing but his shirt. Maybe he did have something to give her after all.

10

"YOU MADE THIS?"

As overjoyed with Phillip's impressed expression as she was with the necklace she'd spent the afternoon crafting, Frankie all but danced in front of him.

"You like?" she asked, trying to sound offhand. As if the first truly gorgeous piece to come from her imagination in months wasn't a big deal.

"It's stunning." He held it up to eye level so the overhead lights glinted off the burnished silver strands, producing a rainbow effect. The orb wasn't onyx as she'd originally imagined it. Instead, she'd used hematite and loved the way the metallic sheen of the gem reflected the silver swirls.

"It's the best thing I've made in a long time. I have the perfect client for it, too," she said, giving up trying to stay calm. Especially since, after texting the potential client a photo, she'd gotten an instant reply demanding an appointment on Monday to see the necklace in person.

"I had no idea this was what you meant when you said you worked in silver." He gently, almost reverently, laid the piece back on the velvet stand, then gave Frankie an assessing look. "Lara's necklace at her wedding. You made that."

Wow, those were some serious observation skills if he remembered what his sister had worn two months ago.

Even though it wasn't a question, she nodded. "It was my gift to her. Most brides would go with pearls or something softer, but she wanted something more, well, her."

"Edgy, sharp and out of the ordinary?" he asked.

He really did remember Lara's necklace.

Delighted, Frankie wrapped her arms around his waist and stood on tiptoe to plant a smacking kiss on his cheek.

"Exactly," she agreed. "Now, we have a bet, don't we?"

"We do?"

"Cookies. If you're blown away by my cookies, we do whatever I want this evening."

"And if I'm not?"

"We do whatever you want."

His hand snaked around her waist, pulling her tight against his body.

"What are the chances we both want to do the same thing?" he wondered.

"I'd say the odds are high," she murmured just before his mouth took hers.

Mmm, he was so delicious.

Her body hummed its appreciation. Oh, yeah, they both definitely wanted to do the same thing. Frankie started to sink into the kiss, then stopped.

Her body protested, lips shifting into a pout at the loss of his mouth.

She definitely wanted him. Wanted to celebrate a great day the same way they'd enjoyed the great night.

But if they did it now, it would ruin her plan.

Operation: Christmas.

Her little thank-you to Phillip for hours of pleasure, for unleashing her creative juices, and, well, because everyone deserved a great Christmas.

She had it all figured out.

But unlike Phillip, she didn't have a contingency plan.

Still, she had to force herself to pull her lips away from his. And even then she couldn't resist another tiny nibble.

"Mmm, c'mon," she said, pulling out of his arms but grabbing his hand. "Cookie time."

"I'm willing to concede if we can keep kissing," he told her.

"Tempting," she said with a laugh, pulling him from the parlor toward the kitchen. "But I spent a lot of time on these, so you have to at least taste one."

"You had time to make that necklace and cookies?" He sounded impressed.

Frankie started to brush it off as if it was no big deal. But dammit, it was a huge deal. She'd made one of the best pieces of her career. One that reflected her taste, showed her vision. She was superstitious enough to believe that if she didn't celebrate it, didn't show her gratitude, then the creativity fairies would snatch the energy right back, making it the last worthy piece she'd make.

Suddenly desperate to show she appreciated him for being her inspiration, she veered in the opposite direction, pulling Phillip with her.

"Where are we going?"

"Your bedroom." She shot a teasing smile over her shoulder. "You can concede I'm the champion there."

He moved so fast, she swore he left smoke in his wake. One second she was laughingly pulling him along, the next he had her against the wall. His mouth ravaged; his hands flew over her body, hot and wild.

She barely had time to think, her body simply took over. Aroused beyond belief, her hands matched his pace, fingers scraping over flesh in her hurry to shove his clothes aside.

Her sweater flew one way, his shirt the other.

His mouth followed the path of her jeans as he swept

them down her legs. Then his lips were on hers again, his rock-hard body anchoring her to the wall.

Panting, desperate, her climax beckoning, she wrapped her legs around his waist.

She had to have him.

Now. Right now.

As if he heard her thoughts, Phillip shifted.

"Now you can concede that I'm the champion," he said just before plunging into her welcoming body.

The instant he slammed home, her body shattered.

Stars exploded behind Frankie's eyes. Her breath came in pants as the orgasm rolled over and over her body.

Just as she started to mellow, as the sensations evened out and her system came back on line, she felt him stiffen. His moves grew sharper, faster. Her body responded, amping up again.

Phillip buried his face in her shoulder and gave a low growl.

Then he came.

Now, that was the way to celebrate, she thought just before going over the edge again.

Two hours, a shower and half a dozen cookies later, Frankie was pretty sure this was the best day of her life.

"You need new furniture." Curled against Phillip on the world's most uncomfortable couch, she tucked her bare feet under her.

"I don't think anyone has ever actually sat on this before," he observed, looking around the antiques-filled room. The television was the only modern thing in it. Which was probably why it had been hidden behind cabinet doors.

"Where did you watch TV when you were growing up?" she wondered.

"At friends' houses? Or if it was something important,

like a presidential address or something, I'd watch in Father's study." He gave her a dry look. "More convenient for the discussion period that inevitably followed."

Frankie's heart ached. The poor guy, he'd never had a chance just to be a kid. To enjoy the simple things in life like a mindless comedy or cookies for breakfast or, well, Christmas.

He needed her.

She could give him all of those things. Fun and joy and simple pleasures.

Not forever, of course.

She knew the novelty of what she had to offer wouldn't hold Phillip's attention for long. But for now...

Her eyes burning, Frankie blinked hard and took a shaky breath.

For now, he needed her.

"Did Lara join in the discussions?" she wondered, trying to keep the conversation light.

"Lara? Of course not. She's female. What would she possibly have to contribute to any discussion about politics," he said in a deep imitation of his father's uptight tone.

"Was he really that bad?" Frankie wondered. She'd always thought so. But maybe he'd been different with Phillip.

"Bad? I wouldn't say he was that. More that he was a man with very firmly held beliefs and expectations. He wasn't abusive. He was a generous provider and an involved father."

"Was he a good father?" Frankie asked quietly.

"I never had reason to believe otherwise. Then again, I met his expectations. Lara would obviously have a different opinion. And with good reason," Phillip admitted quietly. "She called today."

"Lara?" Frankie shifted to better see his face. "How was the honeymoon?"

He winced so painfully she barely managed to bite back her grin.

"Why would you ask that? How would I know? Why would I want to know? Please, don't put those images in my head."

Frankie couldn't help it—she had to laugh and pat his cheek.

"You're a good big brother," she decided.

"Me?" He looked baffled. "Hardly."

"I'll bet Lara would say different."

"After I refused to join her crazy in-laws' holiday festivities? Doubtful."

Frankie wanted to ask why he'd refused. She wanted to believe it had something to do with spending the holidays here with her. But she was a smart girl. She'd just entertain the fantasy instead of asking to have her bubble burst.

She grabbed the television remote off the table. "Ready to enjoy my evening of choice on the world's most uncomfortable couch?" she asked brightly.

He shifted, pulling her onto his lap.

"Better?"

"So much." She sighed.

Twenty minutes later, Frankie was happily transported into her favorite story, but nonplussed by Phillip's reaction.

"I can't believe you've never watched the Harry Potter movies," she said as a brick wall shuffled and transformed into a magical entrance.

"It's a kids' movie," he muttered. "We could watch something else."

"Something that requires a discussion at the end? We can do that with this movie."

"Seriously," he said, setting her on the couch next to him. As if the rock-hard seat would bring her around to his side of the argument. "I don't mind running to the store. I'll pick up a bottle of wine, a few movie selections. I'll even stop by that little pastry shop you mentioned for dessert."

"That's sweet," she decided, shifting to brush a kiss over his chin before grabbing a handful of popcorn. "A sneaky and underhanded attempt to get out of winner's choice, but still sweet."

His sigh was so deep it almost nudged her off the couch.

"Popcorn?" Frankie held up the bowl. She grinned when, in spite of the disgruntled look on his face, he dug in.

By the time Harry put on the Sorting Hat, Phillip was totally engrossed. Frankie enjoyed watching his reaction even more than the movie.

The look of understanding on his face at Harry's shock over receiving gifts during the Christmas-morning scene was so telling.

And it was all the confirmation she needed that her idea to give Phillip the best Christmas ever was a great plan.

"That was actually good," he said two hours later.

"For a kids' movie?" she teased.

"The main characters were kids," he pointed out. When Frankie poked him in the belly, he laughed and admitted, "It was a great movie. Really."

"Great enough to watch the next one?"

"There's more than one?"

Her mouth dropped. Did he live in a cave? Then she saw the laughter in his eyes.

Mission accomplished, she thought with a sigh.

Joy and contentment mingled inside her, filling her with so much warmth.

A night out with a gorgeous man, followed by postdate sex, middle-of-the-night sex and look-it's-morning sex.

A productive day in her studio, better than she'd had in at least a year.

Cookies, dinner and now a cuddle-fest while watching one of the best movies of all time.

She shifted so she was facing Phillip with his arms wrapped around her.

"What would you see if you looked into the Mirror of Erised?" she asked him, referring to the mirror in the movie that showed the viewer his heart's desire.

"Not my dead relatives," he said. His hand slipped under the heavy knit of her sweater, sliding up her spine, then back down again.

"What did you think of Harry's Christmas?" she asked, trying to sound casual. "Poor kid, he'd never celebrated before."

Phillip's hand stilled. His arched brow told her she hadn't been nearly casual enough. But, ever the gentleman, he didn't call her on it.

Instead, he slid around from her back to her front, his fingers slipping under the band of her bra.

"What are you doing?" she asked, instantly aroused.

"Changing the subject," he told her just before taking her mouth.

PHILLIP HAD NEVER understood the concept of a guy being led around by his, well, *manhood* for lack of a better word. Not because he didn't appreciate good sex. He was all for it. But he'd never considered sex important enough to detour from his carefully laid-out plans. And he'd definitely never been so enamored by the act that he'd do something he really didn't want to do just to get it.

Yet, here he was, practically hanging from the rafters. Ignoring his own plans for the day, doing something he seriously didn't want to do.

All because Frankie had put on a pleading look and asked him to help her with the decorations before her grandmother returned.

It wasn't the look that had done him in, he admitted to himself.

It was the fact that she'd been naked at the time.

As he leaned over to hang the light strand on a tiny hook hidden beneath the crown molding, the twenty-foot ladder gave an ominous creak.

"Sent here to give useless talks on the importance of following safety regulations and security," he muttered. "If I fall and break my ass, I'll never hear the end of it."

"I'm sorry, I didn't get that," Frankie called from below.

"Don't you have people to do this?" he said.

"They, um, couldn't make it this year."

He glanced down and sure enough, she was chewing on her thumbnail. He'd come to recognize that as a sign that she was hiding something in that maze of a brain of hers.

"You're not planning to decorate the entire house, right?" he asked, climbing back down the ladder so it could be moved two feet for the next hook.

"Just the foyer for today," she said, giving his cheek a pat. Then, laughing at his expression, she added a kiss. "Come on, admit it. You're having fun."

"No," he said seriously. "I'm not."

"Okay, then, at least admit it looks pretty."

Knowing she wouldn't let him move the ladder until he did, Phillip sighed and made a show of looking around.

It looked nothing like his mother's decorating style.

Oh, he recognized enough of the decorations to know they were the same ones he'd grown up with. But instead of sticking to a single color palette—always the sedate glint of silver in the foyer—Frankie had thrown splashes of color everywhere. Red on the staircase, green around the mirror, a hodgepodge of everything over the door-way and...

Phillip squinted. What in the hell was that?

"That's not ours," he realized, pointing at the four-foot

something guarding the front door. He tilted his head to the side. Maybe it was a reindeer?

"Actually, it is yours," Frankie said, hanging a crystal teardrop from one of the reindeer's antlers. "It was always put out back, though, by the garden shed."

Distracted from the ugly sawhorse with a red nose, he frowned.

"Mother decorated the shed?"

"Nana told me once that this was a gift and your mother didn't want to offend whoever sent it. Once she found a place she felt appropriate—and out of sight—she extended her decorating there."

Which pretty much summed up his family's view of the holidays. It was all for show. All about making the right impression. One foot on the ladder again, Phillip frowned at the string of lights in his hand, then looked at Frankie.

"Why are we doing this?" he asked. "Nobody will be visiting. I promise I'm not hosting some stuffy dinner party. So what's the point?"

"It makes us happy." At the look on his face, Frankie rolled her eyes. "Okay, fine. It makes me happy. And it makes Nana happy. Decorations are a part of the season. Just like those cookies you devoured."

"I'd have devoured them just as fast in July."

"You really don't understand Christmas, do you?" She looked so bewildered, he was tempted to lie just to make her feel butter. But Phillip never lied.

"I understand that for the most part it's a commercial venture that taps into people's competitive nature, puts people into debt and creates a ton of stress." It had even stressed out his mother, whose holiday efforts as far as he remembered had revolved around getting her nails done and telling the cook how many guests would be joining them for dinner.

He hadn't offered his opinion expecting any particu-

lar response, but if he had, he'd have figured she'd either
gasp in horror or smack him for spewing such sacrilege.

Instead, Frankie offered an understanding nod.

He frowned.

"You agree with me?"

"Oh, no. But I know a lot of people who do. That's because they focus on the wrong thing. But people do that
with everything, don't they?"

"What do you mean?"

"Take being a SEAL, for instance." She gestured to him
with her ornament. "Some guys would try to join to boost
their ego, to score with chicks or because they think it's a
great way to bust all over other guys."

"Then they're idiots," he dismissed.

"You've never heard of anyone joining for those reasons?"

"Sure, I have, but guys who think like that rarely make
it out of BUDS. It takes focus, real focus to be a SEAL.
To withstand the stresses and overcome the odds. Less
than twenty percent of the men who try out even make
it through training. The ones who do are doing it for the
right reason."

It took a second for her smirk to sink in. Once it did,
Phillip shook his head. "It's not the same."

"It might be on a different scale, but it's exactly the
same. If you're doing it for the wrong reason, then you're
right, all it does is cause stress."

"Fine," he acknowledged, granting her point. "Then
what do you see as the right reason?"

"Tradition, for one. In our family, even if we decorate
our own tree at our own house, we always meet at Nana's
house on Christmas Eve to decorate her tree together."

"Sounds like a lot of work," he said, eyeing the stack of
ornament boxes with trepidation. She didn't plan on bringing in a tree, did she?

"Okay, how about memories?" She lifted one of the decorations from a velvet-lined box. "There's a note here that says this was given to your grandmother from your grandfather on their first Christmas together."

"Seriously?" Phillip walked over to look. His grandfather had died when he'd been pretty young, but he was the reason Phillip had joined the Navy. "She saved the note, too?"

"No." Frankie handed him the box and the note inside. "He did."

Phillip read his grandfather's spidery script, declaring his devotion to his Audrey on their first of many Christmases.

"I never thought of him as a sentimental man," Phillip mused, remembering the old guy telling stories about the Navy, bitching about the cost of gasoline and always smelling like spearmint gum.

"See, if you'd had family traditions that included decorating with these ornaments, you would have known," Frankie pointed out. She returned the ornament to its box, then put it with a stack of others. "There are more notes. They'll be fun to read while you decorate the tree."

Damn. Phillip grimaced. She *was* going to bring in a tree. He debated protesting, but had the feeling that she'd hide the cookies if he did.

"Are you ready to admit I'm right?" she teased, wrapping her arms around his waist and squeezing.

"Nope."

Her sigh was a work of art, the move pressing her breasts tight against his chest. It was all Phillip could do not to throw back his head and heave a sigh of his own.

He'd never known a woman who could keep him irritated, intrigued and turned on all at the same time.

"Okay, maybe this will convince you that Christmas is special." One arm still around his waist, she fished her cell phone out of her pocket and started flipping through it with her thumb.

"You're going to call Santa?" Phillip guessed.

"Don't think I won't if I have to." She opened the photo album icon and up popped hundreds, if not thousands, of pictures.

"You keep all of these pictures on your phone?" he asked.

"They're not really on my phone, they're in the cloud," she said absently, her thumb flying across the screen in search of whatever it was she thought would change his mind. "Aha, here it is. If this doesn't restore your faith that Christmas brings miracles, I don't know what will."

Phillip peered at the screen, trying to figure out what he was seeing.

"No way." Shocked, he took the phone from Frankie to look closer. "Is that Lara?"

"Yep."

"Smiling?"

"That is indeed a smile."

"Lara, smiling and sitting on Santa's lap?" How was that possible? "Our parents never took us to see Santa. They didn't believe in perpetuating myths."

"That's what Lara told me. I think she was six in this picture," Frankie said. "Your mom left her with Nana because Lara's cold might cause her to inappropriately sniffle or sneeze during some luncheon or other. My cousins and I were with her for the weekend, so Nana took us all out for peppermint ice cream cones, then to see Santa."

"Lara knew he wasn't real. So why does she look so happy?"

"I don't know," Frankie admitted, wishing she did. But she'd only been three at the time. "I remember Nana telling me that Lara said it was a chance to see what magic felt like."

Magic. Believing in something for the simple joy of what it stood for.

The only other time he'd seen his sister smile like that was at her wedding.

"I can text you a copy of the picture," Frankie offered. "You know, for later, after you've talked yourself into believing that I didn't prove that Christmas is special."

"You think you've got me all figured out?" he asked, handing back her phone.

Frankie laughed, the lilting sound filling the foyer, and Phillip's heart.

"No way do I have you figured out," she admitted, tucking her phone into her pocket before linking her fingers together and giving him a soul-searching look. "But I do understand bits and pieces. I know you're an honorable man who's been hurt by others' dishonor. You're a hero who'd scoff at the term. A man who works diligently toward his goals. You give everything to your career but nothing to yourself."

Her words lying heavily between them, she pursed her lips, then gave a little shrug.

"And, of course, you're incredible in bed, you have an undeniable sweet tooth that you keep trying to deny and you are well on your way to having a fabulous Christmas." She flashed him a smile. "How's that?"

"Pretty impressive," he acknowledged. Then, for lack of anything else to say, he drew her into his arms, resting his head on top of hers.

Had anyone ever seen him like she did? Looked inside, past the carefully polished shell, and seen him as a man? One with good and bad qualities, with hopes and dreams. And yes, dammit, fears.

He didn't know if he liked it.

The house phone rang, saving him from having to decide.

"Excuse me." Phillip brushed a kiss over the top of her head before stepping away.

Grateful for the interruption, he strode into the study to answer the call.

"Banks."

"Yo, Banks. It's Evan. Evan Exner. How you doing, buddy?"

"Exner, hey." Phillip dropped into the desk chair, watching Frankie play decorating elf through the open door. "What's up?"

"I heard you were back in town, buddy. I thought you might require my specialized talents."

Phillip frowned, wondering why he'd need advice on smashing beer cans against his forehead. Then he remembered his father mentioning that Exner had joined his father-in-law's real estate firm. His father had also deemed the guy a tactless hack, but that was beside the point.

"You're calling to discuss whether or not I'd like to sell the estate?" Phillip guessed.

"Right you are. So how about it? You available to talk terms?"

Phillip had been planning to sell the estate ever since his parents' death, but hadn't gotten around to actually setting the wheels in motion. In part because he'd never felt right about his parents leaving everything to him and nothing to Lara. He'd actually offered the place to her, but Lara was happily ensconced in California's picturesque wine country.

Still, he hesitated. Not just because his father would roll over in his grave if a tactless hack handled any of the Banks' business ventures. The truth was he wasn't sure he wanted to sell. The house had been in the family for generations, it was close to the Naval Academy, it was paid for. He'd pay more in taxes on the sale than he had in five years' property tax. Lara might change her mind and want it someday.

All bullshit excuses, he admitted.

He glanced at the doorway.

The bottom line was once the estate was gone, so would be any connection he had with Frankie.

And he couldn't stand that idea.

More to banish that thought than because he was ready to commit to anything, Phillip squared his shoulders.

"Sure. Let's meet next week and you can tell me what you think about selling this place."

11

PHILLIP WAS GOING to sell the estate?

Frankie paced from one end of her grandmother's living room to the other, her cussing getting louder with each step.

As soon as she'd overheard Phillip's plans, she'd wanted to scream, yell, and yes, cuss up a storm. But Nana didn't allow that sort of behavior in the Banks house.

So Frankie had hauled it over here, where the worst her grandmother would do if she overheard was tut-tut.

Her grandmother.

Frankie stopped so fast, her feet stuck to the carpet.

If Phillip sold the estate, where would Nana go? Where would Frankie go?

She couldn't afford a place for the two of them. Not yet.

Her jewelry was going well, but it had only been a little while since she'd overcome her block. All she had at the moment were three necklaces, a pair of earrings and a funky picture frame. If she was able to keep this pace she'd have a solid inventory before the New Year. But not enough for first and last month's rent.

Nana had savings, of course. She'd be okay. She could actually retire, travel and have fun like her friends.

For a second, some of the tension drained from her

shoulders as Frankie imagined her grandmother finally relaxing, finally living her life for herself. But Frankie knew that was just a pipe dream.

Nana would never retire, never travel or have fun as long as her flaky granddaughter was struggling.

Nope, she'd tap into her retirement fund to find a place big enough for them both, one that had room for a studio. It didn't matter how long it took Frankie to succeed, Nana would support her—whether she wanted the support or not.

Her stomach churning, Frankie headed for her fail-safe cure-all.

The cookie jar.

She lifted the lid, took a cookie and, after a moment's deliberation, left the lid on the counter. It would just slow her down.

Frankie snapped the head off a frosted Santa, crushing the cookie between her teeth as she paced.

She wasn't going to let her failures ruin Nana's golden years. No way, no how.

Which meant that Phillip couldn't sell the estate. Not yet. Not until she could convince Nana that she'd be fine, that her business was solid.

How was she going to convince him?

She didn't think batting her lashes while naked in his bed was going to work this time.

What would?

Time, maybe? He had to find a good Realtor, she assured herself. No way he'd let a boozer like Evan Exner handle the sale. And a place like the Banks estate was worth beaucoup bucks. It wasn't as if there were a lot of buyers chomping at the bit to take on five acres of fancy upkeep. It would take a while to get it on the market, and even then it wasn't likely the place would sell right away.

Frankie grabbed another cookie, taking a second to contemplate the glittery angel. Oh, Lara. Now that Lara was married, she might want the place. Granted, her husband lived and was stationed in California, but hey. Lara was just contrary enough that she might be an ally.

Feeling a little calmer, Frankie brushed the crumbs off her fingertips and took a deep breath.

Everything was going to be okay.

After all, look at how great the weekend itself had turned out. Almost three days of awesome sex. Great sex. Amazing, even. And that wasn't just her opinion. She knew Phillip was just as blown away by their connection as she was.

Because as good as her cookies were, she knew that wasn't what had convinced him to decorate the foyer with her.

He'd been so cute standing on that ladder.

Grinning, she leaned against the counter and sighed at the memory of him up there, muttering and huffing as he strung the lights.

Cute, and sexy. She sighed at the memory of how his jeans had cupped his backside. She could spend a lifetime with his body and never grow bored.

But it wasn't just about the sex.

He was smart and loyal and strong. He was principled and focused and so, so wounded.

He needed her.

Oh, hell.

Frankie pressed one hand against her stomach, hoping to calm the bats flapping around in there. When that didn't work, she fed them another cookie.

Don't worry so much, she assured herself. Just because she was getting dippy about the guy didn't mean her priorities had shifted. And it wasn't as if she was thinking he'd stick around. The bats were in her stomach after all, not in her head.

She could handle it.

She wasn't going to jump to crazy conclusions. She'd subtly poke around until she found out if he really was going to sell the estate.

And if he was?

She reached into the cookie jar, grabbing two this time.

Obviously great sex wasn't going to keep him from selling the place. But sex had gotten him onto a twenty-foot ladder with a strand of twinkly lights. Maybe if she threw in cookies and a little Christmas charm, she could convince him to wait a while.

Sex, Christmas and cookies. A winning combination if ever there was one.

Wasn't it?

LURED DOWNSTAIRS BY the delicious scent of something baking, Phillip strode into the kitchen. And found something—someone—who made his mouth water even more.

"There you are."

He'd wondered where she'd gone. He'd looked through the entire house before hitting the computer to research local real estate. He hadn't found anything useful, probably because he'd kept thinking about Frankie.

Phillip crossed to the island where she was making something. He didn't check what. Instead, he gave in to impulse and pulled her into his arms. She was still laughing when he took her mouth.

"Mmm, delicious," he murmured when he finally leaned back. He didn't let go of her, though. She felt too good. "Where did you go?"

Something flashed in her eyes, but it was gone before he could figure out what it was.

"I had to get supplies." She tilted her head toward the counter. Phillip's gaze followed and his eyes widened.

"Were you planning to feed an entire platoon?"

"Do you think they'd like Christmas treats?"

"One guy on my team uses cookies as a poker ante. They'd love these," he admitted.

"Then we'll send a box." She shifted, turning in his arms so her backside was cuddled against his front. "What do you think?"

Well, he didn't think he wanted to send his team a box of holiday treats. They'd figure he'd given in to PTSD and gone over the edge.

"I thought you were the cookie queen. I might not be a cookie king, but I'm pretty sure those aren't all cookies."

"Well, when I realized how Christmas deprived you were, I wanted to fix that. That's gingerbread, those are Rice Krispies treat Christmas trees. Pecan tarts, fudge, divinity candy," she named as she pointed to each neat batch. "I picked up supplies for pumpkin, mince and pecan pie too, but I'll let Nana make those."

Phillip's teeth ached and he was pretty sure he felt his pancreas shudder. But he couldn't resist trying a piece of fudge.

"Wow."

"You like?" she asked, shifting out of his arms to give him an expectant look. Even if it had tasted like sawdust coated in gunpowder, he'd have said yes just to keep that smile on her gorgeous lips.

Luckily, this tiny square of culinary bliss tasted nothing like gunpowder.

"I had no idea chocolate could be this good." He, a man noted for his discipline, had to force himself not to take another one.

"Wait until you try my hot cocoa," she said, nodding toward a Thermos.

Phillip frowned at the red plaid vessel.

"I don't think I'm thirsty," he decided.

"You will be after we get the tree."

Frankie amped the wattage of her smile up a notch,

widened her eyes appealingly and did that cute little head tilt he found so adorable.

She was so blatant in her attempt to influence him that he could only laugh.

But he wasn't getting a tree.

"You need to expand your title from cookie queen to dessert queen," he suggested, making a show of looking over the countertop.

"Phillip?"

"The gingerbread looks good, too." He chose a piece at random, popping it into his mouth in hopes that she'd get the hint.

Right.

Hints and Frankie didn't go together.

He didn't have to look over to know she was tapping one booted foot impatiently. He had excellent hearing.

"I just don't see any point in having a tree. I know it's special to you, but I have no attachment to the holidays and I'll be gone the first of the year, so you or your grandmother would be stuck taking down and putting away all that…" He glanced at the boxes labeled *tree decorations* that were stacked against a wall, trying to find a polite word to substitute for *crap*.

"Stuff," he settled on.

"C'mon, Phillip," she said in a tone that was somewhere between sexy and beseeching. He was sure if she used that tone while naked, he'd give her pretty much anything.

His eyes swept over her thick black sweater and thigh-hugging jeans and he all but wet his lips. He knew what was under there and he wanted it. But as long as it was covered, he could resist.

"We'll choose a tree and decorate it together. It'll be fun."

"Frankie, the only thing fun about Christmas is knowing that when it's over there are three hundred and sixty-four days before it has to be faced again."

He didn't think she'd have looked more horrified if he'd told her he was planning a covert mission to take down Santa, blow up the North Pole and sell the elves to cannibals as delicacies.

Which was probably why, three days later, he found himself wrapped in enough snow gear for a trek across the North Slope, carting an ax and a sleigh through the woods—the freaking woods.

"I can't believe you conned me into this," he muttered.

"Conned?" Frankie pressed one mittened hand against her chest and fluttered her lashes. "I did not."

"Yeah. You did. You even roped your grandmother into it." Phillip winced at the memory of Mrs. O'Brian's face when he'd said he'd rather skip the tree. Oh, the guilt. Just because he'd never felt the emotion before didn't mean he didn't recognize it when it pounded through him. He'd tried to ignore it, and had managed for a whole, oh, maybe twenty seconds. Then he'd shrugged, huffed and gone to get the ax.

"Just call us the anti-Scrooge league." Frankie laughed. "Before it's over, you're going to love Christmas."

He rolled his eyes, but it was mostly for show. She was having fun. He'd had no idea how much enjoyment he could get just from watching someone smile.

"This is the best place to cut your own tree," she told him as she stomped through snow up to her knees. "Do you have a preference? Tall and skinny? Short and stout? I like this one, don't you? Although it's kind of lopsided. Maybe if we hang heavier decorations on one side it will straighten out?"

Having never hung a single decoration in his life, Phillip didn't know, nor did he care.

"You should stick to the path," he pointed out. "You're going to be soaked if you don't."

"How can I tell if it's the right tree from the path? Besides, my boots go all the way to my knees. Unless I discover a pothole somewhere, I'll be fine."

Fine. Phillip sighed, watching her bounce from tree to tree like a cheerful sprite. She kept touching the boughs. Rubbing the needles between her fingers. Once she even stuck her face in a tree to sniff it.

"Frankie, we need to get back," he prompted for the fifth time. "Pick a tree, I'll play lumberjack and we can get home and build a fire."

"Are you cold?" She gave him a worried look, her blue stocking cap pulled low over her brow. He started to deny it, then stopped. Hey, it might get her moving faster.

Besides, it *was* cold, dammit.

"Poor baby," she said, hurrying over to the sled. She grabbed the Thermos she'd tied on with the spare rope and gave it a shake.

"I'm not thirsty."

"Maybe not, but you sure are grumpy," she said, unscrewing the lid and filling it with cocoa. If her laugh was any indication, his mood didn't bother her in the least.

"Drink?" she asked, offering the lid. When he shook his head, she drank it instead.

She didn't look offended that he had turned down something she'd made special for this trip. It was oddly freeing, he realized. With Frankie, he didn't have to follow rules or behave appropriately. He didn't have to worry about protocol or meet standards. He could simply be himself.

Which meant that for the first time in his life, he was finding out who he actually was.

A man who was fascinated with a woman who would wear knee-high purple snow boots with a red parka and green mittens. One who'd make cookies for breakfast, put an ugly reindeer in his foyer and entertain him with a children's movie.

His eyes locked on Frankie as she savored the cocoa, and he stepped closer.

He was enamored with her ability to simply enjoy life, the sound of her laugh and, God help him, the feel of her body when he slid inside.

Phillip took the cocoa from her hand and set it on the sled, then, ignoring her startled look, slid his gloved hands around her waist and pulled her close.

And took her mouth.

Their lips danced, his tongue dipping inside to dance with hers.

She was right.

The cocoa was delicious.

Filled with a desperation he didn't understand, Phillip devoured her. Tongues dueled, his hands raced over the slick fabric of her coat, damning winter and all this snow.

He wanted her someplace warm. Someplace he could strip her naked and worship every inch of her body.

"Ahem." Someone was trying to get their attention.

Frankie stiffened, but he didn't let up with the kiss. He was being himself, dammit.

"Excuse me."

Unable to ignore whoever it was any longer, Phillip slowly drew away. His eyes locked on hers, he gave Frankie's butt a quick squeeze before turning to face their interloper.

"Lieutenant Banks?"

Hell. Phillip's body went from aroused to a different kind of stiff in a single glance. He'd just squeezed a woman's ass in the presence of a commanding officer.

"Commander Roberts." Phillip greeted him with a nod. Then, feeling awkward out of uniform and in such a strange setting—none of his training had included what to do if you're caught making out in the woods—he cast around for something to say. "Nice tree."

So much for something to say.

"Right. I hear congratulations are in order," the commander said, frowning.

"Sir?"

"Commander Donovan gave you credit for playing a key role in the planning of his recent mission. Said you're a credit to the team."

Phillip shook his head, not in denial but to clear the ringing from his ears.

Commander? Donovan had gotten promoted? Based on the mission plan Phillip had developed but failed to execute? He hadn't even known the team was back, had no idea how the campaign had played out. But then, why would he?

"Add that to the recommendation on my desk that you be given a commendation for the program you're presenting at the academy, and I'd say you're looking good."

"Sir?" This was beyond surreal. He was standing in the snow in search of a Christmas tree, hearing weird news after bad news from a commanding officer whose stocking cap was covered in dancing reindeer.

Phillip wondered if pressing his fingers against his eyelids would somehow bring his life back into focus.

"As a matter of fact, I mentioned to the admiral that I'd like to see the training program extended."

The ringing turned to a roar that filled his head.

"Stop by my office when you report tomorrow, Banks. I'd like to discuss some options."

With that and an awkward nod to Frankie, the commander gestured with the rope of his sled, indicating the path that they were blocking.

But Phillip was frozen. If the commander had taken that tree, swung it around and beat him with it, he couldn't have been more dazed.

FRANKIE WANTED TO shove the man into the snowbank.

One second, Phillip had been relishing his role as the Christmas Curmudgeon and she'd been enjoying hot cocoa and a kiss. And now this guy had ruined everything.

Since Phillip was doing his best snowman impression, Frankie grabbed the rope of their empty sled and tugged it off the path.

"Merry Christmas," the other man said as he moved around them.

She gave him a narrow-eyed look. He was older, obviously military. He had the look of an understuffed teddy bear. As soon as he passed, Frankie opened her mouth to ask who he was. But she didn't have a chance to.

Snapping out of his trance, Phillip took the sled from her and dragged it farther into the snow. He grabbed the ax, hefted it over his shoulder and stomped over to a tree.

But that's the lopsided one, Frankie debated calling out.

She winced as he started hacking it down.

Not chopping.

Not cutting.

Hacking.

Wood flew every which way like a blizzard before the tree hit the ground with enough force to clear the snow at least four feet. Frankie hurried over to help him lift it, but before she made it halfway there, he'd hefted the pine over his shoulder and headed for the path.

She wondered if he was even going to bother with the sled.

For a second, it looked as though he wasn't sure either. Then he tossed the tree on top, grabbed the rope and tied it down before she'd moved.

He was being a serious jerk. Not in the distant, "I can't believe you dragged me out for this" way he had been earlier. That she'd expected and thought was kind of cute.

Now, not so much.

She'd be irritated with him.

Except she saw how upset he was.

"Here, let me help," she offered, reaching out to help pull the rope.

"I've got it."

Frankie was torn between wanting to give him a hug, to kiss whatever had upset him away and smacking him in his well-muscled arm.

"Let's go," he commanded.

Sir, yes, sir, she thought.

She didn't bother trying to keep up with his pace. If he wanted to do the four-minute mile while dragging a sled and an eight-foot tree, that was his prerogative.

Instead, she meandered along, sipping cocoa and playing back their interrupted kiss in her head. Whatever that commander guy had said had seemed pretty innocuous to her. Maybe it was code. Maybe that was why Phillip was in such a hurry. He had to rush back to save the world. That was the kind of thing he did, wasn't it?

She put the cap back on the Thermos with a frown. It didn't taste good anymore. Either that or the idea of Phillip donning camouflage and facing down dangerous situations was putting a bad taste in her mouth. Her stomach clenched, just like it did each time she imagined what kind of memories were tormenting him.

Not going to think about it, she mentally chanted. *Not even going to wonder.* That scary military stuff didn't fit anywhere in her Phillip-fantasy file.

But he was hurting.

Frankie's brow creased when she reached the parking lot and saw that Phillip had not only paid for and tied the tree to the vehicle but was waiting in the driver's seat with the engine running.

A part of her wanted to scurry back into the woods.

She didn't know how to handle this. How to handle him. Should she try to comfort him? Should she pretend nothing was amiss? Did she ask who Donovan was, why the program being extended was a bad thing?

Nerves jangling, she climbed in the passenger seat.

"Lucky you keep an SUV in the garage," she observed brightly, twisting the Thermos around and around in her lap.

"Right. Lucky," he agreed, pulling out of the farm and heading for the highway. His tone was pleasant and his expression mild.

"I'm here if you'd like to talk," she suggested quietly. "I'm a good listener."

"I don't need to talk, but thank you for the offer."

Frankie wrinkled her nose. He sounded like a robot.

"I figure we should put the tree in the gardener's shed for now, then bring it in tomorrow morning. What do you think?"

"I can take care of it."

"I know you can, but a fresh tree has to be—"

"I'll follow the farmer's instructions and soak the tree. It'll be fine," he interrupted.

She didn't know if he was assuring her or blaming her.

Frustrated and heading toward irritated, Frankie crossed her arms over her chest and frowned.

He didn't seem impressed. Of course, he didn't even look her way so it was hard to tell.

"I'd like to help," she offered through clenched teeth.

"It's a simple process. Take the tree out of the vehicle, put water in a bucket and add the tree. I don't need help."

Apparently not. Frankie swallowed against the tears clogging her throat.

He pulled into the circular driveway.

"What about decorating?" she asked quietly. "What time tomorrow is good for you?"

She saw the answer on his face, so she lifted her hand to stop him before he could blow her off.

"Decorating the tree won't take more than an hour," she assured him as he pulled into the driveway. "We can't just leave it naked. Not only would that be inappropriate for the Banks house, it would be a huge waste."

"Decorate it whenever you'd like," he suggested.

"Not without you." Frankie lifted her chin and gave him her hardest look.

With slow, precise moves, Phillip killed the ignition and turned to face her. He didn't get all flamed up when he was angry like she did. Instead, he turned to ice. His eyes frosted and his expression chilled.

It was kinda sexy.

"I've indulged your whims enough today, Frankie. Now I have things to do."

So much for sexy.

"Whims?" she repeated, her ears ringing.

He sounded so much like his father talking to Lara that Frankie was tempted to look around the vehicle to see if they'd been joined by an uptight prig of a ghost.

"You know, I'm trying to be understanding because you're obviously upset," she said, proud of how calm she could sound while spitting the words through clenched teeth.

"I'm not upset," he contradicted in that same all-important, prissy tone of his. "I am busy, though. So if you'll excuse me, I need to be going."

Translation: "Get your butt out of the vehicle already. I'm done with you."

Who was this man?

Too pissed to care, Frankie threw the door open and

hopped out. She was about to storm off, let him shut his own damned door, and then she stopped.

Turning, she gave him her biggest smile. The one she practiced on snotty saleswomen and her obnoxious cousin.

"After you're finished soaking the tree, you might want to try the same process with your head. That is, if you can find a big enough bucket."

With that and her best flounce, Frankie stormed off.

She didn't make it two feet before she was swept off her feet.

Her scream was drowned out by Phillip's mouth on hers. Gripping her tight, his tongue plunged, plundered and pleasured.

"I'm still pissed," she told him between kisses.

"Okay."

"You were a total jerk," she said as he knotted his fist in her hair.

"Sure."

"This doesn't mean I forgive you," she gasped when he gripped her butt with one hand and pulled her against his erection.

"Nope."

"Let's go inside," she panted. "We can take care of the tree later."

12

CURLED IN PHILLIP'S arms, Frankie didn't know if it had been minutes or hours since he'd carried her up the stairs.

It was all a blur.

One big, sensually overloaded, deliciously orgasmic blur.

She was pretty sure the blur had involved a wall, a dresser and finally the bed. She knew it had included at least three orgasms.

"Maybe there's something to this Christmas thing after all," he'd uttered just before slipping into sleep.

She'd done it. Campaign Christmas was working. Frankie sighed with pleasure.

Even as she slid her thigh along his, reveling in the differences in their bodies, a part of her screamed a warning. This was too much. What he made her feel, how deeply he made her want? It was going to hurt so much when he was gone.

She ran her fingers through the hair on his chest. Phillip's deep, even breathing didn't change.

She wasn't going to worry about it. Not now. She wasn't going to let her fear of tomorrow stop her from enjoying today. She had too much to be grateful for. She had her creative mojo back, was having great sex and enjoying the best holiday of her life.

She was still a little worried about Phillip selling the estate. But no Realtors had come through, no assessors, nothing. He'd even left the reindeer in the foyer. No way he'd let that funky eyesore stay if he was planning to sell.

Frankie smiled, breathing in the subtle scent of Phillip's cologne.

They were making cookies, watching movies and picking out Christmas trees.

Living in the now had some pretty sweet rewards.

Frankie shifted. Before she could slide her body over the delicious hardness of Phillip's, he tensed.

His face tightened, his brow cutting a line through his forehead. She could actually hear his teeth grinding together.

"No. No." His muttered words were filled with excruciating pain, beyond anything she'd ever heard.

Her stomach pitching, Frankie drew back. She wanted to comfort him, but she was afraid to touch him. She wanted to help, but she was terrified that whatever was haunting him would be too much for her to handle. Like a child standing in front of a closet filled with monsters, she wanted to hide under the bed, but knew they wouldn't go away if she did.

Swallowing hard, she tried to steady her shaking hand, then gave up and simply pressed her palm to his chest.

With an anguished howl, Phillip shot into a sitting position, fists up and fury etched on his face.

Frankie screamed, almost falling in her haste to get out of the bed.

What had she done to him?

His eyes glazed, his breath harsh, Phillip hissed through his teeth, then blinked. Frowning, he looked around. When he saw her, he closed his eyes, dropped his face to his hands and groaned.

"Phillip…" she whispered. But she didn't know what to say next.

It was just as well, since he held up one hand to stop her, then slid from the bed to storm into the bathroom. Should she leave before he came out? She was naked, for crying out loud. Her clothes were strewn all over the room and her grandmother was downstairs.

Besides, she couldn't leave him. Not like this.

With a shaky breath, she pulled a blanket off the bed to wrap around her and waited.

She heard water run.

Then he came out.

His hair was wet, water sliding down the side of his neck and over his shoulder. His eyes were bloodshot and his jaw tense. Like her, he'd covered his vulnerability a little by wrapping a towel around his hips.

"I'm sorry," he said, his voice like gravel as he stared out the French doors.

"That's what I was going to say," Frankie told him, keeping her tone light.

He didn't take her invitation to lighten up. If anything his glower deepened and tension filled the room.

Frankie stared at her fingers as they folded perfect pleats into the sheet. She should let it go. She knew he wanted her to. With anyone else, she would. She'd make a joke, maybe drop the sheet and make a proposition.

Ready to do one or the other or both, she pasted on an upbeat smile and lifted her head.

Before she could say anything, her fingers halfway to the knot of her sheet, she froze.

He hadn't moved.

His gaze was locked on the door, but she knew he didn't see the trees beyond. His expression was closed.

His body was so tight he looked like a statue. One of those gorgeous Greek gods, all sleek muscles and tempting lines. Except those statues didn't have scars crisscrossing their backs or climbing from their hands to their shoulders.

Frankie knew he was completely healed.

But Phillip radiated pain. So much pain.

Her eyes filled, but Frankie blinked back the tears. She didn't know what he needed, but she knew it wasn't her bawling.

"I know this is probably one of those top-secret situations that if you told me you'd have to kill me," she said with a shaky smile. A bad joke was better than no joke, right? Since his expression didn't change, she couldn't tell.

"I'm here, though," she said, sliding from the bed. "I'm a good listener."

"There's nothing to tell. I'm fine."

His tone said, *Back off.*

Frankie wet her lips.

He didn't want her help. They were a temporary fling, a good time. Neither of them wanted this heavy emotional stuff between them. Hell, she didn't even know how to do heavy emotional stuff.

So she said the only thing she could think of....

"I love you."

SHE WHAT?

If Frankie had pulled a gun from under that sheet and shot him, Phillip couldn't have been more shocked.

Reeling from the emotional overload of battling the nasty hangover effects of his nightmare, he was tempted to ask her to repeat herself. But he had excellent hearing.

And then there was the look on her face.

As soon as the words had left her mouth, she'd turned so white her freckles almost glowed. Her eyes were huge and her hand slapped over her mouth as though she couldn't believe what she'd just said.

Phillip didn't know what to do with these new emotions racing through him. He wasn't even sure he wanted to identify them. Not when he knew they were the result of a mistaken comment.

She'd been trying to offer comfort. The words didn't mean anything. Not to her.

But to him?

Phillip squared his shoulders, lifted his chin and did the manly thing. He ignored his feelings.

"I'm sorry," Frankie murmured, dropping her hand and scrunching her face. "You sure you don't want to talk about your nightmares?"

Phillip's lips twitched.

He was quite certain this was the first time he'd ever felt like smiling about anything connected to his capture.

"I never confirmed I had nightmares," he said, allowing the subject change. It was the least he could do.

Her grateful smile was like sunshine, chasing away the heavy gray cloud that hovered over his shoulder.

"Alleged nightmares?" she offered, leaning against the bed. The evening light danced across her bare shoulder, her red curls waving over the sheet. Her expression was sweet, but he could see the worry, the concern in her eyes.

He wasn't an emotional man. As he stood in the warmth of that smile, he tried to figure out what it was about Frankie that touched him so deeply. He felt things—things he couldn't label. Things that—like Santa Claus—he knew didn't really exist.

He couldn't address her claim of...well, that claim she'd made, he decided to call it. He wasn't able to repeat her words, even in his head.

But he could assuage her worry.

"They aren't nightmares, simply memories," he told her with a shrug. "Nothing to be concerned about."

"From when you were captured?" she asked in a tiny voice.

"What do you know about that? Did I say something in my sleep?" He was skilled enough to keep his expression calm, his voice even. But his guts were in knots and his heart was tripping as though he'd just stepped on a land mine.

"No," she assured him. "You never talk in your sleep. Heck, you barely even move. Usually the only way to tell if you're having a bad dream is to watch your face. You get this little frown—" she indicated a spot between her brows "—and your body tenses up. Don't worry. You're not giving away military secrets."

"You watch me sleep?"

Her eyes widened. "Sometimes. It's not like I make a habit out of it or anything," she assured him with a wave of her hand. "It's just that I sometimes think about waking you up for a little, you know, sexy time. And I tend to stare a little while I'm imagining how I'll do it."

Damn, she was adorable. Grinning, Phillip dropped onto the bed, patting the mattress next to him. Frankie gave a relieved sigh and sat, cross-legged, to face him.

He arched his brow and waited.

For a moment, she held his gaze, her expression innocent. Then she sighed and shrugged.

"Lara told me. Don't be mad at her, though. She was just venting over something having to do with Dominic. This was after he'd kidnapped her—her words, by the way—and hauled her off to California. I just remember her saying that the reason behind his rude behavior was that he was protecting her because you'd been grabbed by some bad guy while on a mission."

He hated that his sister's life had been put in danger.

That her life had been disrupted, could have been destroyed, because of him. He'd lied to Frankie. Not all of his dreams were memories. Some *were* nightmares in which Lara was the prisoner instead of him.

But he'd never give voice to that horror.

"Rude behavior?" he asked instead.

"I'm paraphrasing," Frankie admitted. "Her actual words were something along the lines of him being a dimpled jackass with a god complex who needed to be taught a thing or two."

"That's Castillo, all right." Phillip laughed. Then, seeing Frankie's smile fade, he sobered, too.

"The mission went bad. We didn't have a contingency plan in place for what happened, and I was grabbed," he admitted.

"How long were you held?" she asked, her words as soft as the fingers she was gently sliding over the back of his hand to trace the paths of his scars.

"Three days. Due to complications, it took the team another two to complete the extraction." For two days, the team had carried his mess of a body through the jungle because they didn't know who the traitor was, couldn't risk a full-scale battle causing an international incident.

A tear slipped down Frankie's cheek.

He wanted to look away, to distance himself from her reaction. He might be able to ignore his emotions, but he couldn't ignore hers.

He turned his hand, joining their fingers together and squeezing.

"Three days..." she whispered. "I can't imagine what it was like, how you felt."

It had been like hell, and beneath the pain and terror, he'd felt the righteous fury of a man who had been sent there unjustly.

But he'd never say that aloud.

"I'm fine. My team is the best."

Phillip gave in to a brewing headache and pinched the bridge of his nose to relieve some of the pressure.

"And yet everything that happened, being captured, being sent here to teach, which you hate… You'd do it all again, wouldn't you?"

There was no judgment in her gaze, no recrimination.

But there was a change. He wanted to ask what she was thinking, why the light in her big brown eyes had dimmed. But he wasn't sure he wanted to know. Instead, he simply answered her question.

"Yes. I'd do it again." He'd do it differently, though. He'd listen to his gut instead of relying on intelligence reports. He'd rely more on his team and less on reports.

He thought back to the meeting in the woods that had set him off this afternoon. If the commander pulled enough strings, Phillip wouldn't have to worry about making those kinds of choices.

He waited for it. The questions, the demands. The pleas. Even his parents, who had fully supported his naval career, hadn't understood his choice to join the SEALs. There were other ways, less risky ways, to advance through the ranks.

But Frankie didn't ask why. She didn't suggest he consider a different career, one that didn't involve the possibility of having his skin peeled off his body. She didn't mention his family fortune, just sitting there gathering interest.

Instead, she gave a deep sigh.

She skimmed her free hand over his cheek, then shifted to her knees so she could lean forward and brush a kiss over his lips.

"I guess that's what makes you special," she said softly.

And just like that, Phillip believed in love.

It was hard not to when he'd just fallen headfirst into it.

FOUR DAYS LATER, Phillip was wishing he could get the same joy out of preparing for Christmas that he got out of Frankie. But it was turning into a serious pain in his butt.

It had taken him an entire day to come to terms with his feelings for Frankie. He'd argued with himself until his face was blue. He'd contemplated the ridiculousness of the concept that love was more than a fleeting attraction, mentally debating the possibility that it could last. He'd even looked up divorce statistics, both in general and in military marriages.

And pondered the data while hanging outdoor lights around the front of the house while it snowed.

But at the end of twenty-four hours, he was still certain he was in love with Frankie, and confident the feelings weren't going to go away.

The next day, he'd debated her feelings for him while listening to his commander offer incentive after incentive in an effort to convince him to request a permanent transfer to Annapolis. Apparently as much as the guy liked the idea of a having a SEAL on staff permanently, he hadn't been able to convince the admiral himself. Not willing to give up, the commander was now calling Phillip into his office daily, hoping to convince him to request a transfer.

Phillip hadn't said no. Not yet.

After all, he might need the job. He wanted to take Frankie to California with him, but he didn't know if she'd leave Maryland. The conservative side of him balked at the idea of living together; his practical side insisted it was too soon, and probably crazy, to live together. He finally deemed it wise to prepare for all contingencies. He'd been at the jewelers when he'd gotten a call from Frankie insisting he had to join her immediately.

He'd paid for his purchase, shoved it in his pocket and hurried to the address, only to be corralled into singing Christmas carols to nursing home residents, then a pediatric wing. Apparently there was something extra festive about a man in uniform singing "Jingle Bells."

He'd worked up a solid dose of irritation, and then she'd thanked him in a very memorable way. He was pretty sure he'd be caroling every December if the tradition included Frankie, chocolate syrup and whipped cream. With or without sprinkles.

And now?

Phillip glared at the string of lights tangled in his hands.

"Why do I always get stuck with the lights?" he muttered. He'd planned to propose tonight. Maybe.

"Don't think I don't see through your excuses and delays," Frankie said, giving him a chiding look.

"What?" How did she know what he had planned? He might be conflicted, but...

Then he realized she was talking about the tree-trimming party she'd lured him to under the guise of an indoor picnic by firelight. It was hard to be upset about it, though, since she was wearing nothing but one of his dress shirts right now.

"If I'd told you we were decorating the tree, you'd have offered up yet another excuse," she said, bending low over the storage container to lift out an ornament. The move hitched the shirt higher on her pale thighs. Smooth temptation backlit by firelight. She straightened and the shirt shifted over her curves, flashing a delicious glimpse of one silken breast. Her eyes were filled with wicked delight, her smile pure temptation.

"You did this on purpose," he said.

"Of course I did. You don't think my grandmother laid out a blanket in front of the roaring fire, chilled the wine and hauled all these decorations in here, do you?" She wrinkled her nose and admitted, "Well, she did haul the decorations in."

"Your grandmother carried these boxes?"

"Some of them," Frankie admitted, hanging the blown-glass sphere from a bough in the area he'd already dangled lights. "I told her I'd do it, but then I got busy in the studio and forgot. I had this inspiration watching the snow fall while we decorated outdoors and came up with a bunch of designs that mimic frost. They look great."

Her decorating had taken place under the roof of the porch, while his was standing on a ladder in that inspiring snow. But since she'd warmed him nicely when he'd come down off the ladder, he couldn't begrudge her the creative success.

"I hate that she's hauling stuff around," Frankie admitted, lifting an ornament out of the box she'd set on a nearby table. "She knows I shut everything else out when I'm in the studio. She should have called me to do it."

"Mrs. O'Brian strikes me as a woman well aware of her own strength." She always had. Phillip untangled the last knot in the strand of lights, frowning as he realized that he couldn't remember a time that Mrs. O'Brian hadn't been here. "Isn't your grandmother close to retirement?"

"Nana? Retire?" Frankie gave a stiff laugh, followed by a dismissive wave of her hand. "Of course not. She loves the Banks house. She'd work here forever if she could."

"Forever?"

"Sure." Nibbling on her thumbnail, Frankie gave him a wide-eyed look. "You know, if you'd let her. Work is important to her and she loves being busy. Having you here, it's been great for her."

There was a frantic edge in Frankie's voice. Was she worried he was going to fire her grandmother? Ship her off to early retirement?

Phillip plugged in the lights and stepped back from the tree. He didn't look at it, though.

Instead, he focused on Frankie's face, which was filled with a sense of peace and pure contentment.

Just like that, the overwhelming anger that had dogged him for months was gone. He searched inside himself, and had to admit that he wasn't at peace with what'd happened. He probably never would be.

But he wasn't fighting the battle any longer.

Phillip leaned against the couch, watching Frankie hang her unique bits of this and that, picture frames and jewelry, baubles and beads.

He'd thought he had it all figured out.

He was a SEAL. He'd carefully mapped out his ascension through the ranks on his way to his admiral's star. His goals had been set in stone for most of his life.

Things were different now.

Now he had to look at all of the facts. Especially where they conflicted with those goals.

Donovan had done a stellar job leading the mission, distinguishing himself enough to nab a sweet promotion. It was a strong contrast to how Phillip had run the very same mission, resulting in his being shuffled here.

He wanted a life with Frankie.

The SEALs didn't need someone like him any longer. But Frankie might. He watched her scatter strands of crystals from branch to bough.

Living here again had never been in his life plan.

But he'd also never planned to be captured by the enemy, be demoted to teaching security classes…or fall in love.

If he'd learned nothing else in the past year, it was that he could adjust.

He glanced at the small box wrapped in purple foil he'd placed on the mantle. The jeweler had assured him that if it didn't suit he could exchange it for something else.

He wasn't ignoring the ring because of nerves or doubts.

No. The timing just wasn't right.

At least that was what he told himself.

Instead, he stepped forward to pull her into his arms.

"What are you doing?" She laughed, her hands locking behind his neck when he lifted her.

"Call it another delay," he said, carrying her to the blanket and reverently laying her in front of the roaring fire.

He wasn't ready to say the words yet. Wasn't sure how to ask for something he didn't understand.

So he'd show her instead.

13

"Mr. Phillip, it's almost dinner time. You get away from those cookies."

Phillip froze, his hand halfway inside the jar. He debated grabbing one anyway, but the habit of obeying orders was too firmly ingrained in him.

"Dinner is in an hour. I've made you a nice beef stew," Mrs. O'Brian continued, bustling into the room with her arms filled with grocery bags.

"Let me help with those," he said, automatically stepping forward to take them.

"Thank you." When she returned to the side door for more, he realized she had a cart she must have wheeled from the garage in order to avoid multiple trips.

"Whoa, that's a lot of food." Before she could start carting them again herself, he moved around her to gather the bags himself.

"There are more bags than usual, but it is the holidays," she told him in a cheery tone.

So everybody kept saying.

"If I eat all this I'll be as fat as Santa," he muttered.

"Is there a problem, Mr. Phillip?" she asked, glancing up from her groceries.

She set a bag of apples and a bag of pecans next to the

sugar and flour. He didn't know anything about cooking, but he was pretty sure he was looking at the makings of an apple pie.

"Nope. No problem."

Still, even if it meant getting the entire apple pie to himself, Phillip was sick of eating alone.

Frankie refused to dine with him more than once or twice a week, saying she was too busy trying to keep up with her ornament orders.

He shoved his hands into his pockets, fingering the box he'd taken to carrying around with him. The pretty paper was getting jacked up, but he figured it was better to be prepared. When the perfect moment to propose arose, he wanted it handy.

He'd never been an indecisive man. All this waffling was driving him crazy. But Phillip figured he'd already blown one of the most important missions in his life. He wasn't blowing this one.

"It must be rough here when nobody's around," he said aloud, watching the older woman hum as she worked. "Boring, I suppose."

"Well, it's not as nice as when you or Miss Lara is home, I'll admit," Mrs. O'Brian said with a smile. "It's usually so quiet here that I don't feel right accepting my salary."

"And I wouldn't feel right if you didn't accept it," Phillip countered.

"Of course you wouldn't. You're a good boy." Her smile was indulgent enough for Phillip to overlook being called a boy at his age. And to sidle over to the cookie jar for a second attempt at a treat. "Still, you might consider other options if you'll be leaving again."

Her words stopped his hand halfway to its goal.

"What options?"

"Oh, you know. A security firm or some such. If you were to visit more often, I could always come in a week or so ahead to prepare the house, stay on during your visit and then close up again afterward," she suggested, folding the last of her canvas grocery bags and tucking them into a cabinet. "Or better yet, have my Frankie stay in the housekeepers' quarters so you have somebody living on the premises. She's a responsible girl and could easily oversee the upkeep between your visits home."

He forgot about the cookies.

"What would you do?" What about her never wanting to leave the Banks house?

His confusion must have come through in his voice, because she gave him a searching look, then shook her head.

"Oh, don't listen to me. I was just thinking out loud. Feeling guilty over having such a wonderful home and pay and doing so little to earn it." She waved her hands as if shooing her earlier words away. "I know your parents' will was clear. I'd never ask you to make any changes."

What did his parents' will have to do with her retiring?

Before he could ask, the doorbell chimed.

"I'll get the door," he said, grateful for a chance to review the conversation and figure out what had been said. As fast as he could, he grabbed a couple of cookies to take with him, offering a rueful smile of apology on his way out.

It was the best he could do since his mouth was full.

They were addicting.

Every time he ate one, he thought of Frankie.

Probably because it was her that he was addicted to. He pulled open the front door, expecting to see Evan Exner, full of hope of changing Phillip's mind about the sale of the estate.

He was hoping to see Frankie.

But no...

"What are you doing here?"

"Hey, Phillip," Lara said, tucking her arm under her husband's. "Surprise."

He damn near shut the door again.

Ten minutes later, he was wishing he'd gone with that impulse.

"What do you mean you're here for the holidays?" he asked.

"I didn't think it was a very complicated statement," Lara said, looking around the parlor with enough interest to tell Phillip that she didn't remember spending time in here any more than he did. "We—that would be Dominic and I, if you weren't sure who I meant by 'we.' Here—that would be the house, obviously. And since you've got some serious decorations going on, you already understand the holiday part. Love that reindeer, by the way."

Phillip clenched his jaw and strove for control. He wasn't going to let her mock him.

After a second, he slid his gaze to the large man taking up half of the antique chesterfield.

"You used to her smart mouth yet?" he asked.

"Every time I think I am, she pops off with something that surprises me," Castillo admitted. "Look, it's no big deal. Since she's spending Christmas week with my family, Lara decided it was only fair that we spend this week with you."

"A week?" he squeezed out. A whole week?

"A whole week," Lara confirmed, reading him clearly. And, if her wicked grin was anything to go by, she was enjoying the spot she'd stuck him in. "Maybe a week and a half, depending. Castillo has to report back on the fifteenth but I might stay on."

Why? Phillip rubbed the bridge of his nose and reflected fondly on his life six months ago. Everything had been just about perfect then.

"My old bed is on the small side," Lara pointed out.

"You don't mind if I bounce on a few others, find one we like?"

"You okay with this, sir?" Castillo asked. Whether he used Phillip's call sign out of habit or because he couldn't figure out what to call him in this setting, Phillip wasn't sure.

"Yeah. Sure." Phillip waved his hand in the air. "Bounce away."

Lara snorted.

Castillo grinned.

Phillip sighed.

"Thanks for your permission," Lara said, angling herself off the couch. "Is Mrs. O'Brian here? I'll let her know we're staying, see if she can cover us for dinner."

"She's in the kitchen." Phillip hesitated, then, figuring he deserved something given the circumstances, called after her, "Bring back some cookies."

"Right." She laughed.

And left the two men alone.

He wanted to call her back, tell her he'd get the cookies.

He didn't want to be stuck here alone in the room with Castillo.

Not because he didn't like the guy—although the jury was still out on that. But because Castillo represented the world Phillip wanted, needed. And felt as though he'd been thrown out of. Seeing the other man opened doors Phillip had closed. Jeopardized the control he thought he'd regained.

He wanted to ask about the mission. To confirm that Valdero had been caught and punished, was maybe frying in hell that very moment. He wanted details, corroboration on his suspicions about the traitor. He clenched his fists and shoved them into his pockets to hide the telltale tremors of anger that had overtaken him.

He wanted enough details to see it in his mind, to live it. He needed the closure those images would bring.

But he didn't ask.

Because it was against protocol.

He'd spent his entire life following protocol. And for what?

Grabbing on to control as though it was a lifeline, he shoved the fury back into the corner it had claimed in his mind.

Instead, he tried to think of something to say. But all he could come up with were inane comments about the weather.

"Dude, this couch sucks," Castillo observed.

"So I've been told." Grateful that the ice had been broken, even if it painfully reminded him of Frankie, Phillip inclined his head. "It sounds as if you have a busy month ahead of you."

"Wasn't my idea." Castillo grimaced. "Going home for a few days, just before and after Christmas? That would be great. But a week, week and a half? Holy hell."

Phillip frowned.

"I thought you liked your family," he said without thinking. Realizing how rude that sounded, he added, "That was my impression, I mean. That you and your family were close. You always spend the holidays at home."

"Yeah, but this gives my sister and cousins all that time to talk to Lara."

Phillip's frown turned to a scowl. What was wrong with talking to his sister?

"And that's a problem because…?"

"They tell her stuff. Stories, gossip, every embarrassing thing that's happened in my life. I swear they mine the rest of the family for dirt to dish." The other man shook his head in disgust. "It's bad enough when it's just my sister. But she'll have accomplices. Wily ones. A week with them will undo months of charm, you know?"

"I'm sure it won't change Lara's feelings," Phillip murmured. But Lara telling Frankie stories? He didn't know that his sister had any, but he wouldn't put it past her to share what she knew. And he wasn't sure enough about Frankie's feelings to take a chance.

Of course, he still wasn't sure enough about Frankie's feelings to propose either.

"You know, I'd always figured you grew up in a place like this. Snobby and rich, with extra fancy on the side." The other man looked around. "Turns out it doesn't suit you, though."

His gratitude over the subject change had only lasted as long as it had taken Castillo to finish talking. Phillip frowned. Was that a compliment buried in there?

"Not saying it's not nice," the guy added. "It just reminds me of a museum."

"Most museums are more comfortable," Phillip muttered before catching himself. "Can I get you a drink?"

"Pretty sure that's what Lara was getting," Castillo reminded him.

Lara, who should be back by now if that was all she was doing. Since she wasn't, he figured there was a reason.

Meeting the other man's watchful stare head-on, Phillip waited to hear it.

"Donovan got promoted. Rumor is he's being recruited for DEVGRU." DEVGRU, or Special Warfare Developmental Group, dealt primarily in counterterrorism and was considered by many—including Phillip—to be the elite of the elite.

And it had been Phillip's most coveted ambition.

It was like getting a punch to the gut.

Fast, painful and numbing.

"His performance on this last mission pushed him

over the top?" Phillip asked, wanting confirmation that the mission he'd carefully planned and nurtured in hopes of getting just that opportunity had worked—even if for someone else.

"Doubtful. He refused to take credit. Gave that all to you, as a matter of fact."

"Me?" Nonplussed, Phillip shook his head. "That's crazy. He led the team while I was here playing scout leader to a bunch of green midshipmen."

"True that. But he pointed out that you'd planned the mission—both times—and that you were the one who'd fingered the mole. Guess he didn't feel right taking credit when he was just a stand-in." Castillo pursed his lips and added, "The rest of the team was pretty much unanimous in their agreement."

Phillip had once been slammed in the head by a submarine hatch that had left his eyes spinning and his ears ringing. This was pretty much the same feeling.

Donovan had given him props. Not just to the team, but to command. It wouldn't erase the black mark captivity had put on his record, but it might balance it somewhat.

And that, Phillip realized with a surge of gratitude, was a good way to go out.

Overwhelmed, he looked away.

"So...scout leader?" Castillo mused, sliding lower on the couch in search of a more comfortable spot. "Did you have them tying knots and making parachutes out of old skivvies?"

HER BELLY FULL OF good food, mellowed by wine and great company, Frankie followed Phillip into the parlor.

It was the first time she'd seen him as a SEAL. Watching the interaction between him and Dominic had been enlightening. They seemed to speak in code, to read each other's intentions and expressions without needing words.

She wasn't even sure if they liked each other, but they were a team and had complete trust that the other would have their back.

Was that why Phillip was so devoted to being a SEAL? Because in spite of everything that had happened to him, everything that could happen, he knew his team would always be there?

Her breath hitched in her chest, tears flooding her eyes. They would be, wouldn't they?

Not going to think about it, she promised herself fiercely. She deliberately shifted her thoughts to Phillip and his sister.

"You know, the way you and Lara poke and tease each other, nobody would know you two had been apart for, what is it? Eight, nine years?"

"More like all our lives," he said with a shrug. "And I think it was more Lara who was doing the poking and teasing."

"You go ahead and tell yourself that." Frankie laughed and watched as he knelt down to start the fire in the fireplace. Someone had already lit the lights on the Christmas tree, its decorations gleaming a wonderful contrast of elegant and funky. She loved the look of her ornaments mixed in with Phillip's—the effect not too stuffy, not too quirky. She tilted her head and sighed. Yeah. It was just right.

Sort of like everything else in her life right now.

The holidays were here. Her nana was happy; Frankie was surrounded with good friends. And an incredible lover.

Her business was booming, the jewelry designs flowing from her imagination as easily as they had before her block. Instead of taking orders now, though, she was uploading each piece to her website as soon as it was finished. They were selling almost as quickly as she uploaded them, but she knew that was partly due to the holidays. So she was playing it smart this time, still putting in a few hours a day on her ornaments. With that in mind, she'd designed a Valentine's frame that would be fun enough to personalize and produce in large quantities. She already had a few dozen orders.

She felt like herself again. Inspired and excited…and content.

The contentment was new. And all due to Phillip.

She was crazy in love with him.

She watched him take a moment to check the fire, as if to ensure it would obey his command and flame beautifully. It did, of course.

Then he stood and turned.

The look on his face wiped the smile right off hers.

It was so intense. So serious.

And it scared the hell out of her.

Then she noticed the wine bottle chilling next to two flutes.

Her heart did a slow dive into her toes.

It was all so romantic.

Too romantic. Like, goodbye romantic.

"Wine?" he offered.

"Sure." She suddenly had a feeling she was going to need it.

While he poured, Frankie sat on the couch. She shifted from one cheek to the other, then got up to fiddle with one of the ornaments that wasn't hanging quite right.

It wasn't as if she hadn't known he was leaving. Of course he was. His assignment was temporary—and he hated it. He lived for being a SEAL. She'd known that before, but watching him with Lara's husband had cemented that fact.

They were temporary. A fling. Hot, wild sex with the questionable bonus of falling in love.

"Frankie."

She took a deep breath, turned and accepted the glass

he held out. She wanted to sit. She really wanted to run. But she stood and sipped instead.

"I've made some decisions, I'm making some changes," he told her. He looked as serious as if he were explaining that the Grinch had just stolen Christmas and all the cookies in the world. "I wanted to share them with you first, and then ask you a question."

Frankie quit sipping and took a big gulp instead.

"I've been asked to transfer to the academy. I have a great deal of knowledge that they'll benefit from."

Frankie's jaw literally dropped.

"That means I'd be leaving the SEALs. Not quite that simply," he said, frowning into his glass. "But under the circumstances, it can be done."

She opened her mouth to ask why, to tell him he was crazy. But all that came out was a wheezy breath.

"I'll live here in the house, of course. I know it's an anachronism of uptight living, but it can be made comfortable. New couches, a little color." His smile was so sweet it melted her heart. "You'd have fun with that, wouldn't you?"

"Me?" she said, the word barely making it past the knot in her throat.

"I'd planned to set the scene, maybe something romantic." He looked around the room, the Christmas lights twinkling softly and the candle flames dancing. "But I figured this suited you better. Suited us better."

Delight seeped through the nerves tying knots in her belly. She stared, her eyes so huge they watered, as he pulled a small box from his pocket. The purple foil was wrinkled and scuffed and the ribbon askew. But it was the most beautiful box she'd ever seen.

Frankie blinked.

She had to. Her eyes, and reality, insisted on it.

She had to stop him.

Before he took off the paper, before he handed her the box, before she saw what was inside.

She had to stop him now.

"Phillip, no."

"What?" Brow furrowed, he looked at the box in his hand, then back at her. "I don't think you understand."

"Yes," she insisted, backing away so fast she almost fell into the tree. She set her glass down with a *clink,* and was afraid she'd chipped the pricey crystal. "I know what you're doing, what you're asking. But, please, don't."

"Why?" The word was as toneless as his impassive expression. This was how he'd dealt with the horror of his captivity, she realized. He'd retreated inside himself, closed off. And now she'd made him do it again.

Oh, man, she sucked.

"You'd give up everything," she tried to explain. "A career you love, a warm climate with sand instead of snow. You'd move back here to a house you hate, take a job that will make you miserable. How can I say yes to that?"

His expression eased a little, his eyes softening.

"You're here," he said simply. "Your business, your grandmother."

Her business, which was now handled almost exclusively online. Her grandmother who wanted to retire but wouldn't because her granddaughter was a flake.

Frankie's heart wrenched, aching so much she wanted to cry. As much as she wanted to tell him that, to say she'd go with him instead, she couldn't. Because as much as moving here would ruin his life, her moving west with him would never work out.

"We're not forever, Phillip," she said softly. "We're temporary. A little out-of-character fun."

"What's that supposed to mean?" His expression was closed now, his body stiff.

She hated to do it, but she thought it best to hurt him a little now rather than a ton later.

"You've said it yourself, more than once," she told him sadly. "This is out of character for you. All of this has been an aberration for you."

"What are you talking about?"

"You don't do Christmas, Phillip, yet you're decorating for the holidays. You don't like this house, yet you're planning to live in it." And the worst. "You hate your assignment, but you're going to make it permanent."

A little voice in her head screamed at her to shut up. His choices would make her life so much easier. So much better. But they'd ruin his. And Frankie loved him too much to do that.

"Those are my choices to make," he said, as if reading her thoughts.

"I'm not your type," she tried instead.

"What's my type?"

Someone who would love him enough to accept his dedication, to understand his moods and to bring fun and joy into his life. Someone who would make him happy, who would give him peace.

Oh, this was so hard.

Frankie lifted her chin and called on every bit of her strength. She had to play it just right. Otherwise she'd break down and cry, throw herself at his feet and cling to him like a parasite, holding on until she'd drained him of life.

"You're the type who's always looking out for the long term, Phillip. Everything in your life has been built around your goals, around your future."

"So?" He stood now with his arms crossed over his chest and that look on his face. The one that reminded her of his father. "There's nothing in that statement that explains your reaction."

"I don't do long term," she explained quietly. Ignoring the pain as her heart crumbled, she gently touched his arm. "I'm temporary, Phillip. I'm ice cream for breakfast, calling in sick to have sex all day, blowing off commitments because something else feels better." She pulled her fingers away, instantly missing his warmth. "I'm crazy impulses, instant gratification and try, try again."

"So? Why are those bad things?"

"They aren't. They just don't fit you. Not in the long term."

"You're being ridiculous."

"Maybe. Which should prove my point." Frankie's fingers danced over the Christmas tree. She sent one glass ball spinning and looked at Phillip. "Your decorations are priceless heirlooms."

She flicked the silver snowflake she'd made, sending the tiny hearts jingling. "And I'm quirky and unconventional."

"Why don't you finish with these ridiculous comparisons?" he snapped. "And tell me the truth. Why are you turning me down?"

"I'm turning you down for your own good." Frankie gave a bitter laugh. "That doesn't feel any better to say than it does to hear. But it's true. You're supposed to be a SEAL. You're meant to lead, to command. Not to teach."

"Things change. I'll be an asset to the academy."

"Maybe. Probably. But you won't be happy," she said with a morose shake of her head.

For a second, he looked baffled, as if a career and happiness had nothing to do with each other.

She was so tempted to say yes.

She wanted so badly to try.

But she couldn't.

She'd spent half her life obsessing over her fantasy Phillip. He was her escape, her inspiration.

And if she said yes, she'd be the reason he left behind the most important thing in his life.

Besides, she just wasn't strong enough, confident enough to handle the real-life Phillip. The SEAL whose mission it was to save the world. Not long term. Not when she knew she'd end up letting him down.

Besides, she was his fantasy girl. *His* escape. Their time together wasn't his real life. She was happy, so happy, that she'd given him something special, something so wonderful that it made him think he'd be happier with her than he would be achieving his lifelong goals.

Her heart ached, misery seeping through her.

Because she knew better.

Sooner or later, he'd hate her.

Being with him, pretending they had a chance, might be worth it.

She'd love every second of it.

Except for the part where she ruined his life.

"I've got to go," she said, turning blindly.

He didn't say a word.

He didn't have to.

His pained silence was enough.

14

HER LOWER LIP SHAKING, Frankie sucked in a deep breath and pounded on the door with all her might.

Nothing.

She pounded again.

A moment later, she heard an impressive litany of bitching before the chain slid loose and the door swung open.

"This had better be life or death," Shayla warned, her blue hair standing out at odd angles.

"Phillip wants me to marry him," Frankie said. Then she burst into tears.

Thirty minutes later, she was curled up in the corner of Shayla's couch, surrounded by time-tested, girlfriend-approved heartbreak remedies. A box of fine chocolates, a bowl of salty chips and a bottle of cheap wine.

"Navy boy asked you to get hitched?"

"He started to," Frankie admitted through her sobbing hiccups. "I wouldn't let him finish."

Shayla leaned back on the couch with a contemplative look.

"So what's the deal? The guy sucks in bed?"

"Phillip?" Frankie snorted into her glass. "Hardly."

"He's a jerk? A bigot? A sexist? He hates kids? He kicks animals? He's mean to your grandma?"

"No, no, no. Hardly, never and you're kidding, right?"

Shayla pulled her kitten-appliquéd robe over her knees and gave Frankie a hard stare.

"It's midnight and I have to be to work at six. If this doesn't get good soon, you're outta here."

"That's mean." And just in case she meant it, Frankie downed her wine in one swallow. "And so was what Phillip did. He ruined everything."

"By asking you to go marry him?"

"Yes!"

"The bastard."

Frankie rolled her eyes, but Shayla's sarcasm had the intended effect. It made her feel like enough of an ass that she stopped crying.

"We were doing great, you know. We had fabulous sex. I actually managed to get him into the spirit of Christmas. We had more incredible sex. I baked him cookies and made him smile. We talked, we watched movies, we had even more mind-blowing sex. We connected, you know?" She blew out a breath, hoping it would relieve some of the pressure in her chest. "I was so happy with him. And I think I made him happy, too."

Quite a feat, she figured. Phillip was many things. Upright, dependable, strong, focused, sexy as hell. But he had never been happy. She'd changed that. Before she'd made him miserable, of course.

"Hmm, it sounds like you guys would be a mess," Shayla agreed. "After all, all you had between you was an amazing connection and incredible sex."

"Quit making me sound stupid." Frankie scowled.

"Quit giving me material."

Fine. Her legs still folded underneath her, Frankie leaned forward on her knees to refill her wineglass, grabbing the chips while she was upright.

"Fine. So we had a lot going on. Why ruin it?"

"Isn't he supposed to leave the first of the year?" Shayla asked, nibbling on a cookie as if taking tiny bites would stop her from eating more.

"Is that any reason to get married? Just because he's supposed to go back to California?" *Supposed* to. "That's a big commitment to make because of a few thousand miles between us. Isn't it?"

"Well, I'm the queen of transient relationships, so I can see why you'd think that's the answer. But temporary relationships only work under certain circumstances."

"What circumstances?"

"The people involved aren't in love."

Frankie's bottom lip trembled. She stared into her glass, wishing the wine would make everything look clearer. Had she made a mistake?

"He's a SEAL," she muttered. "He's one of the best. I mean, he's like a supersailor best. He fights terrorists, he rescues hostages." *He gets captured.* Frankie didn't say that, though. It might be a secret, and she couldn't betray Phillip by saying something she shouldn't.

"Oh, I get it," Shayla said, heading into the kitchen. "He's all about his career, right?"

He was supposed to be. He should be. Guys like him, who were that good, the world needed them.

But Frankie couldn't admit all of that unless she also admitted that as amazing as he was, he'd offered to give it all up for her.

So she gave a jerky nod instead and shoveled a handful of chips into her mouth. Maybe food would help her churning stomach.

"I understand." Shayla popped open another beer, then gestured with the can. "When I fall in love, the guy had better put me first. I want to be his entire world."

But if she was his entire world, he'd depend on her. He'd

trust her like he did his SEAL team. But unlike his team, she wasn't sure she'd be able to always be there for him.

"Remember that lead guitarist I dated?" Shayla mused, plopping back on the couch and handing Frankie the box of chocolates so she could take the chips. "Totally dedicated to being a rock star. I'll bet a Navy SEAL is even worse. He'd be gone all the time, right? Doing all sorts of top-secret stuff he can't tell you about."

"I suppose he'd be gone sometimes. But from what Lara says, it's not a ton. Not nearly as much as your guitarist when he went on tour."

"No? Okay." Shayla wrinkled her nose. Then she shrugged and crunched another potato chip. "But I'll bet your SEAL is, like, totally obsessed. He probably spends all his spare time doing work stuff. He'd be busy doing push-ups and would probably forget to come to dinner."

Frankie frowned as Shayla's image twisted and turned in her head.

"You know, I'm pretty sure if Phillip was doing push-ups, I'd forget about dinner, too." He had the kind of body that put the thought of food right out of a girl's head. "Besides, I do the same thing. I get crazy focused when I'm in the studio, you know that. I don't take chances with inspiration. If a piece is going right, I work on it until it's finished. You never know if the vision will be the same the next time you grab your tools."

Shayla puffed out her bottom lip and gave Frankie a steely stare.

"You're not doing this right. We're burning this guy out of your heart, remember?"

What? Frankie replayed that statement a couple of times, then shook her head. "That doesn't make any sense," she finally decided.

"What do you expect from me after midnight? Brilliance?" Shayla frowned, and then shrugged. "So put in less creative but more understandable terms, I'm trying to help you get over the guy. I can't do that if you don't work with me. We're supposed to list all the reasons the relationship sucks, then trash him for a while. You keep countering my trash by defending the guy and I'm gonna have to ask why you aren't home either packing your bags or jumping his bones."

"Can we trash me instead?" Frankie looked up from the chocolates to give her friend a tremulous smile. "I'm the problem."

"Come again?"

Frankie tossed the candy onto the couch and dropped her face into her hands with a long groan.

"He's ready to give up his career for me. He loves being a SEAL. But all he talked about was living here, transferring to the academy." Frankie raised her head to give Shayla a horrified look. "He'd give up the SEALs, he'd give up California for me. He hates the snow."

For a long moment, she just stared. Then Shayla rubbed her forehead and gave a pained sigh.

"I'm confused. You are totally crazy about this guy. He's the best thing since cordless vibrators. He wants to marry you." She waited for Frankie's reluctant nod and shrugged. "I'm not seeing the issue. He sounds pretty great to me."

"It is. He is. But I don't deserve a guy like that. I don't stick with things, Shayla. I'm a flake." She thought of all the reasons she'd given Phillip and nodded. "A total flake. I can't make a relationship—a real one—work with Phillip. He deserves a woman who is just as dedicated and focused as he is. One who'll always be there to take care of him. Who will put his needs first instead of using him for sex and inspiration. He deserves a great woman. One who's perfect for him."

For one second—one blessed second—Shayla just

stared. Then she exploded. Frankie winced as the chips hit the floor when her friend flew off the couch. Shayla paced the room, arms flailing in the air, cusswords flying.

Then she stopped in front of Frankie and pointed.

"You're doing it again. I've told you time and again that you do this, but you keep denying it. And now here you are, waking me up, doing the same damned thing," Shayla said accusingly, her finger aimed like a weapon. "Any time you want something—really, *really* want it—you build it up into this huge production in your head. Then, once it's the size of—oh, let's say impossible—you think you have to change yourself into something else, someone else, for it to work."

"I don't do that," Frankie muttered.

"You did it with your jewelry." Shayla gave a triumphant nod. "It was great as it was, you were loving what you were doing. But as soon as you hit some invisible milestone, you acted like you had to change or it would all be ripped away from you."

"A smart businesswoman has a business plan, has goals and benchmarks and controls," Frankie defended.

"Was your goal ever to be a businesswoman?"

Her mouth open, her argument right there on the tip of her tongue, Frankie went blank.

"What?"

"What is your career goal?" Shayla said, stretching the words out.

"To be a successful jeweler."

"So why didn't you ever measure yourself by the success of your jewelry? Instead, you started raking in orders, taking on jobs you didn't like and working yourself into a breakdown. Then when you burned out, you beat yourself up."

Pressing her lips tight to keep from throwing up, Frankie shook her head. Shayla nodded.

It took three swallows before she could clear her throat and ask, "Why?"

"I think you're afraid," Shayla said softly. "Dreaming is easy, you know? Thinking about how great things would be, planning, that's fun. It's like a big, shiny carrot keeping you moving forward. But doing is different. It's a commitment."

She'd done the same thing with Phillip, hadn't she? When he'd been fun to dream about, exciting to chase, everything had been fine. Oh, sure, she'd worried a little about the heartbreak to come, but those thoughts had been easy to push away in the midst of the exhilaration and thrill.

Frankie knuckled away a tear.

"Here's the thing," Shayla said quietly. "You blew up your career, but you're still making jewelry. So what happens if you go for this, and it blows up?"

A million possibilities, each more melodramatic than the last, flashed through Frankie's mind. But she knew there was only one real answer.

"I love Phillip. That won't change, no matter what." She took a deep breath, the nerves suddenly settling in her stomach. "And if Phillip loves me, it won't matter what I do to blow things up. He'll be there to fix them."

PHILLIP WAS AN expert at many things.

Marksmanship. Strategy. Electronics.

He'd never claimed to have an inkling of expertise when it came to women. But damn, he'd never felt so stupid.

Since attempting to wash away his feelings of ineptitude in the shower hadn't brought any enlightenment, he got out. Ignoring the mirror, he grabbed a towel and strode into his bedroom.

He still didn't understand Frankie's argument. So they

were different. Why was that a bad thing? Who the hell wanted to be with someone exactly like them?

It was a testament to how lousy he felt that he left the towel where it fell.

Clad only in boxers, he automatically reached for his uniform, then stopped, staring blankly into the armoire.

He couldn't remember what day it was. Did he have to report today or not?

Before he could remember, his door flew open.

And in strode hurricane Lara.

"Do you mind?" he snapped, grabbing the first thing he touched. Denim. Looked as if he was going casual today.

"Nope, not at all," she said, bouncing around the room, her expression filled with curiosity. It was probably the first time she'd ever been in his room, he realized. "Where's Frankie? I thought she'd be here."

"In my bedroom?" Giving up hope that Lara would take the hint, he yanked the jeans on.

"Are you trying to say you and Frankie haven't been doing the horizontal mambo?" she asked with a grin.

"I'm saying that's none of your business." He grabbed a shirt and yanked it on.

"You better add a sweater. It's freaking cold here." She shivered, glaring out the window. "Was it always this cold? I don't remember."

He shrugged. He couldn't remember either.

"You stopped by to bitch about the weather?"

"I told you, I'm looking for Frankie. We were supposed to meet this morning, but she's nowhere to be found."

"Her grandmother's?"

Lara rolled her eyes. "Like I wouldn't try there first? Nowhere to be found means not the house, not Mrs. O's house, not the grounds, not the pool room. Nowhere."

"Why are women such a pain in the ass?" Phillip pinched the bridge of his nose.

"Aha. There is something going on." Lara stopped prowling his bedroom to poke her finger at him. She put enough force into it for him to almost feel it from across the room. "What's up?"

"Doesn't your husband want you?"

"Always. But he's out." Lara stepped closer, her expression conflicted. Phillip recognized the look. He'd seen it plenty of times in the mirror. She wanted to reach out, but God forbid things get emotional.

Phillip pulled the sweater over his head, as much to buy time as because, dammit, it really was cold here.

"Frankie took off last night," he said, running a hand over his already dry hair. It was longer than it should be. "I, um, was in the process of proposing and she took off."

"You were proposing…marriage? To Frankie Silvera?"

"Yeah."

"Seriously?" Lara rocked back on her heels, considering his words. Then, damn her, she gave a delighted laugh. "That's awesome."

Phillip stared.

"Do you hate me that much?"

"Hate you?" Looking horrified, Lara shook her head. "Of course not. You're my brother. Since that finally means something to both of us, why would you think I'd hate you?"

"Oh, I don't know. Maybe your taking pleasure in my suffering?"

Lara dropped onto his bed—uninvited, of course—and rolled her eyes.

"That's not hate. That's love. This is good for you."

That was it.

The final straw that broke his control.

He actually heard it snap.

He sent the socks in his hands flying across the room like a missile. Then he sent the dresser after them. He had a chair in hand, ready to heave it, too, when he saw Lara's face.

She didn't look scared. She didn't even look surprised. She'd pulled her legs up, wrapped her arms around them and sat with her chin on her knees, watching patiently.

It was the patience that cut through his fury.

Mostly out of surprise.

"I didn't know you could do that," she said when she realized he was finished.

"Lift a dresser?"

"Lose control."

"It's been a hell of a year." With a bitter laugh, he dropped onto the bed next to her.

Lara laid her hand over his. After a second, Phillip was unable to resist turning his hand and entwining his fingers with hers.

"Look, what you went through sucks. No question about it. For some men, it'd be the end of their career. Hell, most guys I knew before Dominic would have curled up into a ball to cry, then hidden in some safe closet for the rest of their lives."

She laughed when Phillip sized up the armoire.

"Nope, you won't hide. You're not that kind of guy."

Maybe he was. He looked down at their hands and grimaced. He'd used his feelings for Frankie as an excuse to rush both of them. Instead of giving her time, giving them both time, and waiting until he was sure of what she wanted, he'd pushed. Not because of Castillo's warning that sisters had big mouths. But out of his own intense need to return to his team after seeing the lieutenant. His need, and his fear that when he did, he'd fail again.

Damn. He heaved a deep sigh. That was a lot of weight to put on a proposal. Was that why Frankie had run? Or was her refusal still one of those female mysteries?

Like the one sitting next to him.

"So why is Frankie turning me down a good thing?" he finally asked.

Lara grimaced and shrugged so that her chin-length hair swayed gently.

"From school to sports to your career, you've had everything easy, Phillip. I'm not saying you didn't earn your successes. But you didn't suffer too many setbacks either." Lara glanced down at their entwined hands, her thumb tracing one of the scars on his. "Now you have."

His ears buzzing, Phillip could only stare at his sister.

The fury wasn't new. It was as familiar as his own skin now.

But the shock of what his sister said had him blinking.

He'd been betrayed by a trusted ally, captured and tortured. His spotless record was blown, his clean ascension up the ranks shot to hell. He'd offered his heart to a woman for the first time in his life and had it handed back to him with a look of pity and a smile.

That was what she called those things? Setbacks?

Then it hit him.

She was right.

He'd ignored his own strategy, and instead of looking at contingencies, he'd thrown up his hands in surrender.

"Setbacks suck," he decided.

"Yep, totally," she agreed. "But they aren't endings unless you let them be."

With that and a quick kiss on his cheek, she left.

Phillip had to smile.

Who knew his little sister was so damned smart?

His smile faded when the door closed.

He'd had two setbacks. Frankie and his career. But if he tried to reclaim one, didn't it mean having to give up the other?

He'd thought his capture had changed him.

And it had. For the worse.

He'd been sure no woman could change him.

But Frankie had. For the better.

Lara was right. Setbacks weren't endings. He'd make sure of it.

HER STOMACH BOUNCING between her toes and her throat, Frankie forced herself through the doorway and into the foyer of the Banks house.

And almost ran right back out.

Maybe this was a bad idea.

Maybe she should give Phillip time to not be pissed at her.

Maybe she should come back later.

With cookies.

Then she saw that someone had draped a wreath around the reindeer's neck. And the cockeyed, crooked bow told her *who* that someone was.

He was so sweet.

And apparently psychic, since he chose that moment to walk in.

Oh, baby, he looked good.

"Everyone has been looking for you," he said, not appearing surprised to see her. He didn't seem angry, hurt or upset either. He looked totally calm, completely mellow.

Should she pout?

"I'm sorry. I had to…" What? Run away? Prove that she was the inconsiderate flake she'd claimed? "I meant to be back earlier, but I wasn't feeling well."

"Are you sick?"

"Junk food hangover," she admitted, wondering if he'd ever had one. The baffled expression on his face said no, but that could just be because he wasn't sure why she was in his house.

"Can we talk?" she asked quickly, before he could suggest she turn around and leave. Not waiting for his response, she automatically headed for the parlor.

Her feet froze on the threshold. Wasn't this like returning to the scene of the crime? Maybe they should talk in the kitchen. There were cookies there. Or better yet, his bedroom. She turned, running straight into Phillip's hard chest.

"I thought we were going to talk."

"Um, yeah, let's talk." She'd rather stay here, curled up against his warm body. But she was supposed to fix things between them.

She walked over to the tree, her fingers dancing over the ornaments. His and hers, side by side.

She'd fixed Phillip's outlook on Christmas.

She could fix this, too.

Taking a deep breath, her chin up, expression bright, she turned to face him. Seated on the couch, he had one leg crossed over his knee and a patient look on his face.

She almost melted at the look in his eyes.

Love. She was sure that was what she saw there.

"Look, um…" She wet her lips. This was hard. *Just blurt it out,* she told herself. "I changed my mind."

Phillip gave her a narrow stare, clearly looking for the catch.

Frankie knew what it was, but she wasn't saying. Not yet.

"You've changed your mind," he repeated, drawing the words out. "About my proposal?"

Frankie twisted her hands together, and her rings cut into her flesh, she was gripping so tight. But she was afraid to let go.

"Yes. About that."

"That…" Phillip leaned back on antique couch, looking as casual as if he were talking about the weather. But

the expression in his eyes told her that the weather had the potential to quickly turn very unpredictable.

She waited for him to explode.

But he didn't. Instead, he gave a friendly nod and smiled.

"And the list of reasons we're completely unsuited that you shared yesterday?

"It's still valid." She frowned. "Of course, it was valid when we first met. And when we first slept together. And it'll still be true one year from now or ten."

"So you admit it was pure bullshit?"

Frankie's mouth dropped.

"Well, not pure, I mean…" She grimaced.

Phillip grinned.

It was that smile that did it. It was as if he'd opened the floodgate, and suddenly everything she'd promised herself she wouldn't tell him started spewing from her mouth.

"I was afraid, okay. I was terrified I'd ruin this, ruin us. You have no idea what it's like to feel like a failure," she shouted. "To want something so badly you can taste it, to see it so clearly in your head you swear you could touch it. But when you reach out for it? Nothing. Because you've blown it."

Frankie shoved her hands through her hair, tugging to relieve some of the pressure building inside her head.

"I spent years perfecting my craft. I gave up dates, blew off friends, lived on ramen noodles and peanut butter to build my business. I busted my ass, Phillip. I wanted that more than I wanted my next breath. It was everything to me." She had to stop. The tears were coming so fast her words were a blur. She took a shaky breath, determined to finish this. "The dream wasn't stolen from me. Nobody lied or cheated or screwed me over. I couldn't make it work. No matter how much I wanted it, no matter how important it was to me, I couldn't hold on to it."

She finally looked at him again, and then wished she hadn't.

His expression was about the same as she'd expect if she'd dropped a grenade in his boxer shorts. Horrified disbelief combined with a hefty shot of fear and a whole lot of irritation.

Phillip got to his feet, obviously about to say something. Frankie held up her hand to stop him.

She had to finish.

He deserved that.

Poor guy.

"As much as my career meant to me, as important as that dream is, it's nothing compared to how I much I love you," Frankie confessed quietly.

Staring at the polka dots on her rain boots, Frankie waited. The urge to cry was gone.

Replaced by an urge to throw up.

"Say something," she muttered when she couldn't stand it any longer.

"I'm trying to decide where to start."

Before she decided if that was a good thing or a bad thing, he was right there in front of her. Her stomach jumped. Damn, he moved quietly.

Frankie lifted her gaze, but before she could check his expression, he kissed her. Hot and sweet, his lips moved over hers. The fear that had been knotted, tight and painful, in her belly broke loose. Frankie had no idea what the kiss meant, but she knew it had to be good.

Didn't it?

Unless it was a pity kiss.

Frankie groaned.

Phillip leaned back.

"That wasn't a sound of pleasure," he observed. "Did you think up more reasons why we're wrong for each other?"

"Well—"

"I think it's my turn," he interrupted, brushing his lips over hers before stepping back. "You've laid out the obstacles. I'll cover our advantages."

"We have advantages?" Setting her nerves aside—not too far in case she needed them again—Frankie dropped onto the couch from hell, ready to be convinced.

"I'd say we do." Phillip faced her, legs spread and hands clasped hands behind his back. "For every difference you stated that we have between us, I can counter with a similarity."

She tried to school the "yeah, right" out of her expression, but she wasn't that good of an actress.

"We both like cookies. We enjoy the same music and sports, and while we haven't watched a lot of the same movies, experience tells me that once we do, our tastes there will mesh, as well."

He paused, arching one brow.

Frankie shrugged. Those were "go on a first date" similarities at best.

"To continue," he said, doing just that, "we both have affection for my sister and your grandmother. We dance well together, and we're incredible in bed."

He considered that for a moment, and amended it to, "We're mind-blowingly in sync, totally in tune and perfectly suited for each other sexually. Be that in bed, the kitchen, the backseat of the car or a shower. I have no doubt that as time goes on we'll prove that there isn't a single location that we have sex in where we're not amazing."

A giggle bubbled in her throat, but Frankie swallowed it back.

"We haven't had sex in the backseat of a car," she pointed out.

"We can remedy that after we finish this discussion." The promise was made with a look so hot that she could only hope the car was in the garage. Otherwise, anyone who glanced out one of the front windows of the house was going to get a show.

"Phillip…"

"We have similar world views, enough differences to keep things interesting and enough stubbornness to ensure that whatever choice we make, we'll stick with it."

Frankie's heart ached for him. He was trying so hard and she knew he'd never had to work—let alone work this hard—to convince a woman of his interest.

But she was afraid it was only because of that stubbornness he spoke of. And she knew firsthand that when something wasn't working, stubborn simply wasn't enough.

"And I understand failure," he said quietly. "I've tasted it up close and personal. It can eat you alive if you let it. Or it can be, well, a setback. Something you deal with and move on from."

Frankie wanted to reach out, to press her hand against his cheek and give him an understanding kiss. She wanted to assure him that he wasn't a failure—he was a hero.

But as usual, seeing her intention, he gestured for her to wait.

"As important, or unimportant, as all of that may be," he said quietly, "the bottom line is I love you."

"Ooh." Her eyes filled. Pleasure rushed through her with fear sliding in right behind. Frankie bit her lip. She wanted to believe him. She wanted to assure him that she believed they had a chance. She lifted her chin and opened her mouth to say just that.

"Is that what they call standing at attention?" she asked instead. She added a bright smile to the question as an apology.

"No, this is at ease."

"And are you?"

"At ease?" At her nod, he shrugged. "I'm trained to

handle high pressure, to excel under duress and to only react after careful consideration of the circumstances."

"So that's a no?" Frankie's smile turned real.

"That's a no," he confirmed.

And that was all it took to convince her that whatever challenges they faced, however many differences they had, they'd make it work.

"Good," she told him, getting to her feet. "Because I love you, too."

His eyes widened before he closed them and gave a relieved sigh. When he opened them again, Frankie was right there, ready to dive into his arms.

He drew her close.

"You know, the first time a guy says *I love you* to a girl, he shouldn't say it as though he's issuing a command," she told him, brushing kisses over his face between words.

"No? Well, I've never done this before. What's the protocol?"

"He should wrap her in his arms."

Phillip's arms tightened around her shoulders and her waist, his hands warm on her back.

"He should look deep into her eyes, give her a mind-blowing kiss and then he should say it."

His brows arched as he considered her instructions and then nodded.

Settling on the couch with her comfortably in his lap, he cupped her face in his hands, lifted her chin slightly and stared into her eyes.

Frankie's heart melted at the sweet sincerity in his green depths.

"I want to spend my life with you," he told her, brushing a gentle kiss over her mouth.

Oh, there was the catch. Frankie's pleasure dimmed a little.

"You want to spend your life here?" she asked.

His expression didn't change. But she felt the slight shift in his body. As if he was bracing himself.

"I'm a SEAL. I belong with my team. I want you to come to Coronado with me. We'll keep this place." He tilted his head to indicate the house. "Your grandmother can retire, or semiretire, or move into my parents' room. Whatever you want. But you and me, we're going to be together."

Oh. He was so perfect. Her eyes filled with tears of joy. This was so perfect.

"I love you," she whispered through the tears. Frankie cupped her hands over his, turning her head to kiss one of his palms.

"I love you, Francesca. You are like sunshine, brightening my days, filling my heart with warmth. I need you. In my life, in my bed, in my heart."

"Yes," she said, laughing and crying at the same time. "Oh, yes. I love you so much."

His eyes filled with the same joy she was feeling, Phillip grinned. Then he leaned forward.

"Never let it be said that I can't follow orders," he murmured just before his mouth took hers again.

* * * * *

REQUEST YOUR FREE BOOKS!
2 FREE NOVELS PLUS 2 FREE GIFTS!

HARLEQUIN®

Blaze®

red-hot reads!

YES! Please send me 2 FREE Harlequin® Blaze™ novels and my 2 FREE gifts (gifts are worth about $10). After receiving them, if I don't wish to receive any more books, I can return the shipping statement marked "cancel." If I don't cancel, I will receive 4 brand-new novels every month and be billed just $4.74 per book in the U.S. or $4.96 per book in Canada. That's a savings of at least 14% off the cover price. It's quite a bargain. Shipping and handling is just 50¢ per book in the U.S. and 75¢ per book in Canada.* I understand that accepting the 2 free books and gifts places me under no obligation to buy anything. I can always return a shipment and cancel at any time. Even if I never buy another book, the two free books and gifts are mine to keep forever.

150/350 HDN F4WC

Name _____ (PLEASE PRINT) _____

Address _____ Apt. # _____

City _____ State/Prov. _____ Zip/Postal Code _____

Signature (if under 18, a parent or guardian must sign)

Mail to the **Harlequin®** Reader Service:
IN U.S.A.: P.O. Box 1867, Buffalo, NY 14240-1867
IN CANADA: P.O. Box 609, Fort Erie, Ontario L2A 5X3

Want to try two free books from another line?
Call 1-800-873-8635 or visit www.ReaderService.com.

* Terms and prices subject to change without notice. Prices do not include applicable taxes. Sales tax applicable in N.Y. Canadian residents will be charged applicable taxes. Offer not valid in Quebec. This offer is limited to one order per household. Not valid for current subscribers to Harlequin Blaze books. All orders subject to credit approval. Credit or debit balances in a customer's account(s) may be offset by any other outstanding balance owed by or to the customer. Please allow 4 to 6 weeks for delivery. Offer available while quantities last.

Your Privacy—The Harlequin® Reader Service is committed to protecting your privacy. Our Privacy Policy is available online at www.ReaderService.com or upon request from the Harlequin Reader Service.

We make a portion of our mailing list available to reputable third parties that offer products we believe may interest you. If you prefer that we not exchange your name with third parties, or if you wish to clarify or modify your communication preferences, please visit us at www.ReaderService.com/consumerchoice or write to us at Harlequin Reader Service Preference Service, P.O. Box 9062, Buffalo, NY 14269. Include your complete name and address.

HB13R2

SPECIAL EXCERPT FROM

HARLEQUIN *Blaze*®

New York Times bestselling author
Vicki Lewis Thompson is back with another
irresistible story from her bestselling
miniseries *Sons of Chance!*

A Last Chance
Christmas

She stood on tiptoe, wound her arms around his neck and gave it all she had. So did he, and oh, my goodness. A harmonica player knew what it was all about. She'd never kissed one before, but she hoped to be doing a lot more of this with Ben.

Although she'd never thought of a kiss as being creative, this one was. He caressed her lips so well and so thoroughly that she forgot the cold and the late hour. She forgot they were standing in a cavernous tractor barn surrounded by heavy equipment.

She even forgot that she wasn't in the habit of kissing men she'd known for mere hours. Come to think of it, she'd never done that. But everything about this kiss, from his dessert-flavored taste to his talented tongue, felt perfect.

As far as she was concerned, the kiss could go on forever. Well, maybe not. The longer they kissed, the heavier they breathed. His hot mouth was making her light-headed in more ways than one.

That was her excuse for dropping her phone on the concrete floor. It hit with a sickening crack, but in her current aroused state, she didn't really care.

Ben pulled back, though, and gulped for air. "I think that was your phone."

"I think so, too." She dragged in a couple of quick breaths. "Kiss me some more."

With a soft groan, he lowered his head and settled his mouth over hers. This time he took the kiss deeper and invested it with a meaning she understood quite well. Intellectually she was shocked, but physically she was completely on board.

This time when he eased away from her, she was trembling. Like a swimmer breaking the surface, she gasped. Then she clutched his head and urged him back down. She wanted him to kiss her until her conscience stopped yelling at her that it was too soon to feel like this about him. "More."

Pick up A LAST CHANCE CHRISTMAS
by Vicki Lewis Thompson,
on sale December 2014,
wherever Harlequin® Blaze® books are sold.

When it snows, things get really steamy...

Wild Holiday Nights

from Harlequin Blaze offers something sweet, something unexpected and something naughty!

Holiday Rush by Samantha Hunter

Cake guru Calla Michaels is canceling Christmas to deal with fondant, batter and an attempted robbery. Then Gideon Stone shows up at her door. Apparently, Calla's kitchen isn't hot enough without having her longtime crush in her bakery...*and* in her bed!

Playing Games by Meg Maguire

When her plane is grounded on Christmas eve, Carrie Baxter is desperate enough to share a rental car with her secret high-school crush. Sure, Daniel Barber is much, *much* hotter, but he's still just as prickly as ever. It's gonna be one *looong* drive...and an unforgettably X-rated night!

All Night Long by Debbi Rawlins

The only way overworked paralegal Carly Watts gets her Christmas vacation is by flying to Chicago to get Jack Carrington's signature. But Jack's in no rush to sell his grandfather's company. In fact, he'll do whatever it takes to buy more time. Even if it takes one naughty night before Christmas...

Available December 2014 wherever you buy Harlequin Blaze books.

HARLEQUIN®

Blaze®

Red-Hot Reads